The DAZE BEFORE Christmas

LAURIE GERMAINE

Scattered Whimsy

Published by Scattered Whimsy 2024

This novel is entirely a work of fiction. The names, characters, and incidents portrayed in it are the work of the author's imagination. Any resemblance to actual persons, living or dead, events or localities is entirely coincidental.

Printed in the United States

First edition

ISBN: 978-1-7371977-5-1

Cover designed by GetCovers.com

Acknowledgement clipart designed by freepik.com

To Mom and Dad

Thank you for blessing me with

a foundation anchored to the

Solid Rock.

Author's Note

Kris Kringle/Meister K is the Santa Claus from my *Tinsel in a Tangle* duology. He makes a few cameos in this book, but you needn't have read my previous works to enjoy this story.

Prologue

Santa's Village (Flitterndorf)

A KNOCK sounded on the oak door to his office, and Kris Kringle looked up from his worktable. Gadgets and gizmos and toys in every stage of assembly littered the tabletop. "Come in."

His secretary, Frau Bericht, poked her head around the door-jamb. "Sorry to disturb you, Meister K, but your grandson is here to see you."

"Oh? Please, send him in."

She withdrew, and the door opened wider as Niklas entered, carrying his two-year-old son in one arm and a red envelope in his other hand. "Hey, Grandpop. Gram sent me over with this." He held out the envelope, crimped and worn with age. "Tinsel and the baby are napping, and this little man has too much energy to play quietly, so I thought we'd visit the Workshop and run Gram's errand at the same time."

Kris reached for his great-grandson rather than the envelope.

"Set that on my desk, please." He bounced the boy on his knee, and Kole's chubby hands clutched his beard. "Your grandmother showed you the 'Unanswered' file box, then?"

"Yeah. I had no clue you kept letters that long." Niklas moved past the table to the desk positioned by the picture window. "It's one secret after another with you."

Kris winked at Kole, and the toddler giggled.

"Although, I'm surprised there weren't more unanswered letters in the box, given the number of believers in the world."

Kole yanked on his beard, and Kris winced. "Most letters get answered on their own without my help. Others need the refinement of time before I step in."

"The refinement of time? Is that how you explain the letter I saw dating back to the 1980s?" Niklas returned to help untangle Kris's beard from Kole's little fist. "I'm sure whoever wrote it forty-plus years ago—"

"Ah ah. That is a special case. One I suspect you might have the pleasure of witnessing for yourself."

"Witnessing. Not answering?"

Kris handed Kole back to Niklas without comment.

Niklas chuckled. "Another secret? Fine, I won't pry—this time." He lifted his son atop his shoulders and moved toward the door. "We're off to the Production Wing. I promised Kole he could watch the delivery train make its rounds." Niklas ducked through the doorway so his son's head would clear the casing. "See you at dinner."

"Dinner. Yes." As the door clicked shut, Kris rose from his stool and reached for the letter Niklas had delivered. He smoothed a thumb over the bare, top right-hand corner and removed the letter dated almost ten years ago.

> *Dear Santa,*
>
> > *I know, I know, it's too early to be writing you a letter—we're only in late February!—but this is*

important. You'll be pleased to note I've already gone to the Big Guy Upstairs, but since I doubt He's listening to me these days (I don't blame him), I'm hoping you can help me. Then again, you might put me on the Naughty List for life after what I've done.

Here's the thing: Cash Cooper is an amazing guy and comes from an amazing family, and he deserves to be with an amazing girl. He thinks I'm that girl, but deep down, I know I'm not. And if I let him convince me otherwise, the truth of who I am, what I am, would end up staining the unblemished canvas of his life.

I can't let that happen! So, I took measures into my own hands and made sure he witnessed me kiss another guy at the high school Valentine's dance when I was supposed to be his date. He can't stand cheating. But how else could I prove that he's wrong to waste his emotions on someone like me? In time, he'll see it's better we go our separate ways.

This is where you come in, and why I'm writing early. All I want for Christmas is for you to help Cash find a new girl. One worthy of his love, one he won't regret having chosen when he's old and gray. I know you specialize in toys, but many movies suggest Santa also deals with matters of the heart. Surely those movies can't all be wrong.

You've come through for me in the past, ~~Gra~~ Santa. Thanks for helping me out in this too. You're the best!
  Sincerely,
  Hadley Jacobs

Kris lowered the letter as a band of pressure settled across his shoulders. The same pressure he'd experienced when he'd first received her Christmas wish years ago. A tragic case, that Hadley

Jacobs. An understandable, yet dissatisfying, ending. But hope often rose from the Yule log ashes.

Pursing his lips, Kris turned to the picture window and peered down at the snow-blanketed, elfin village below. Wisps of smoke curled from the chimneys, and several young elves practiced hockey on the outdoor ice rink. He shifted his focus upward to the afternoon sky where, this far north, stars had already emerged for their daily trek across the heavens.

"You think now is the time to answer Hadley's letter?" he asked.

The brightest star winked at him, and Kris sighed. "Of course, You would ask this of me during my busiest three weeks of the year. Not that I'd be gone the entire stint, but …" He ran a hand down his beard in thought. His intermittent absence this Christmas season might be a good test for his son, Nico, since Kris hoped to retire in the next couple of years.

Grinning at the sky, Kris Kringle, a.k.a. Santa Claus or Father Christmas or Babo Natale—he answered to whatever the children called him—let out a deep *Ho, ho, ho.* "All right, I'll do it. Where are You sending me this time?"

Chapter One

Boston, MA, December 2

GWYNN SADLER sat at the wide checkout counter of Gilded Editions with a recent shipment of glossy photographs: America's iconic movie stars from the '50s through the '80s. Holding up the print she'd just matted, she shook her head at Paul Newman wearing a cowboy hat.

"You look way too hot in that Stetson," she admitted aloud in the empty art gallery.

Paul Newman could probably make a sweatsuit look dreamy, but Gwynn drew the line when it came to an American western hallmark like the cowboy hat. Except, this time, the way Newman's pale blue eyes popped beneath the wide brim made the concept of that hat halfway … appealing.

A memory tickled at the fringes of her mind, but she squelched it before faces and tender feelings could manifest. She slid the matted print into a clear plastic sheath, folded over the opening, then taped it shut and put Newman face-down atop the growing pile of other prints slated for the sales floor.

"Is this another hint, Lord?" She glanced at her almost-but-not-quite finished canvas painting sitting on the easel nearby. It beckoned her with a mix of revulsion and infatuation. "First You inspire me to paint a western landscape, and now I'm intrigued by a Stetson. Well, whatever You're trying to tell me, I'm not interested."

As Dean Martin crooned the lyrics to "White Christmas" over the gallery's speakers, Gwynn took the next print—a much safer one featuring Marilyn Monroe—and adhered it with mounting strips to a fresh mat board. She glanced at the oversize "Tree of Life" clock on the wall to her left, its branched hands showing two hours until closing. Could this day go any slower?

After slipping the Monroe print into a plastic sheath, Gwynn stacked it atop Newman, reached for another print … and peeked again at her canvas painting. Her fingers itched for her paintbrush as much as her heart loathed the setting she painted.

"Why now, God?" Gwynn asked, and then followed through with an eye roll. She really needed to stop talking out loud, even though her last customer had left Gilded Editions an hour ago. Currently, she worked alone, preparing prints for sale, dusting framed artwork, and trying to look professional and competent until her boss returned from an extended lunch break.

"You may take your break when I come back," Irene Burns had said before the door chimed shut behind her.

Gwynn's tummy had since growled itself to exhaustion. If necessary, the granola bar in her handbag from who-knew-how-long ago would ward off starvation.

The wind picked up outside, pelting the early December rain against the shop's awnings above the windows. Boston locals and tourists hurried along the sidewalk, heads down, hands cinching their jackets closed at their necks. A few sipped hot drinks. Others wrestled with umbrellas. Still others spoke into their phones.

What a raw afternoon. Gwynn shivered in the spacious gallery as she matted another print. This historic brick building may be the envy of many entrepreneurs, but it bled heat like watercolor bled on paper. She'd rather be at home curled up on her sofa, snug in a wool sweater, homemade butterscotch candies on hand, the flames dancing in her fireplace as she watched cheesy Hallmark Christmas movies.

Okay, so "home" meant the apartment she shared with two suite mates, Mia Burke and Holly Monroe; their sofa listed to the right, Gwynn's one wool sweater sported holes the size of quarters, she'd eaten her last candy three days earlier, and their fireplace? Electric. Yep, fake flames.

Gwynn hopped from her perch on the metal stool, gave a tug on the jacket of her navy blue pantsuit, and grabbed the protected prints she'd readied for sale. As she arranged them in a cloth bin near the front windows trimmed in pre-lit garland, she caught sight of her professional looking reflection and sighed.

"*You're* a fake," she said, smoothing a wisp of bottle-blonde hair back into her French twist. "Fake prestige. Fake successes. Fake life. Your artistic talent might as well be fake too."

Conviction nicked her heart, and she flinched. "Sorry, Lord. Thank you for the redo. I don't mean to complain. I just thought …" She'd thought her life would look different by now.

Some would call her young at twenty-four, but the fact that she was single, had no children, and could focus solely on her career … well, didn't that mean she should have already carved out a significant niche for herself among the other artists in the city? She *had* promised Uncle Russ—

"Ugh, snap out of it, Gwynn." She whirled away from the windows and narrowly missed toppling into Irene's three-foot Santa Claus positioned near the entrance. One hand was raised in greeting, and a wire-framed lighted reindeer stood at his side.

Gwynn scowled. Christmas, she loved. Santa, on the other hand, had fallen from her good graces years ago. The only reason he held a prominent spot in the gallery was because Irene, despite being a self-proclaimed Grinch, had learned customers relinquished their credit cards more readily this time of year if she catered to their holiday whimsies.

"Jolly fat man, my foot," Gwynn grumbled, striding back to the checkout counter in her Jimmy Choo knockoffs. She yanked her pleather handbag from the shelf beneath, withdrew her phone, and tapped into her text thread with Holly.

Help! she typed. **Pity is here to party and I didn't give it permission!**

A moment later, Holly replied, **That's twice in one week. Do we need to go shopping tomorrow to cheer you up?**

Tomorrow's Sunday. You know I don't shop on Sundays.

Next Saturday, then. *I* could use the pick-me-up.

Gwynn shook her head. **I can't. The art show's next weekend and Irene needs my help.**

Oh, right. The prison warden has you chained all day.

Her thumbs flew over the keypad. **Irene's not THAT bad. And I enjoy selling art.**

You like CREATING art.

"Hard to create when one is blocked," Gwynn murmured as she typed the words.

Then pick a day for shopping so we can unblock you! Holly shot back.

The front door chimed as a broad-shouldered man sporting a well-trimmed white beard, red plaid jacket, and thick black boots entered. He shook out his umbrella, water droplets flying in all directions.

"Anywhere but on Irene's murals," Gwynn whispered, as if speaking the words could redirect the raindrops.

Gotta go, she texted. **Customer.**

Said customer chuckled at Irene's Santa Claus, his own stocky frame dwarfing the three-foot mannequin. "It never gets old," he muttered, giving one last shake of his umbrella before folding it up.

Gwynn slipped her phone into her bag and smiled at the elderly gentleman. "Hello. Welcome to Gilded Editions."

The man nodded, gesturing with his umbrella toward the windows. "A drizzly day we're having, *nicht wahr*?" His deep voice had a Sean Connery flair (Mama Edith loved those James Bond movies), but Gwynn blinked at the foreign words.

"Neesht what-now?"

Smiling, the man waved aside her question and turned in a circle. He looked from the sizable glass-framed pictures hanging on the walls to their smaller, less expensive unframed duplicates grouped in bins around the showroom. He grunted then frowned.

Gwynn linked her hands in front of her and took a few measured steps toward him. He seemed familiar in a distant-relative kind of way. "Are you looking for anything in particular? I might be able to steer you in the right direction. Do you like landscapes or cityscapes? Classic or modern? Retro? Vintage? Animal? Mineral? Vegetable?" Gwynn cringed. *Lord, make me stop.*

With a throaty chuckle, the old man peered at her. "Are you the artist?"

"Of these paintings? No, sir." Not yet. Someday. Someday this shop—and similar galleries nationwide—would sell her works.

Provided she could revive her withering creative juices.

"I thought not." The man clasped the umbrella behind his back. "No soul in these."

"Excuse me? Gilded Editions represents over a dozen artists in and around the Boston area. Why, my boss—"

"I'm sure they'll make fine eyesores—excuse me, *art*—in someone else's stuffy foyer. But what I need is—" His gaze shifted over her shoulder and his eyes twinkled. Yes, *twinkled.* She threw the Santa mannequin a suspicious glance as the man brushed past her to stand in front of her canvas painting. "This. I need this."

Her eyebrows hiked. "But it's not finished."

"Isn't it?"

The painting depicted mountains and rangeland in the background with a lone ranch house and weathered wooden fencing in the foreground. But the colors in the sky looked wrong, and she hadn't adequately captured the house's aura.

"No, it isn't," Gwynn said.

"But this has soul," the man argued. "Character. A hint of pain. Maybe longing."

Gwynn swallowed. Who was this guy?

He turned to her. "You may not have created those … um … pieces"—he indicated Irene's artwork hanging on the walls—"but you *are* an artist, yes?"

"On my good days."

"Then you know the emotion that goes into paintings such as this one." He cocked his head at the canvas again. "What do you think, did the artist create this from his or her imagination, or from an actual place?" He stroked his beard. "Or a combination? Reminiscent of the Rocky Mountains, I think."

"How do you figure that?"

"The aspen trees. The mountains' jagged slopes. A wooden fence instead of a stone wall." He winked. "How am I doing so far?"

Gwynn schooled her features into nonchalance. "I wouldn't know. I see nothing but a forsaken house and rotting wood."

The man tsked. "And you call yourself an artist."

"I said on the *good* days."

"Every day you draw breath is a good day."

Her cheeks heated. "Yes, sir."

The man wagged the umbrella at her painting. "You know what this is missing?"

Gwynn shook her head.

"People. Not a crowd, mind you. Just a few amiable folk. A couple embracing. Or a family on a picnic. Cowboys on horses?" The man gave a merry chuckle that sounded oddly like a *ho ho ho.* "That would go with the American West vibe I'm picking up. People make the world go 'round, don't you think?"

"Sorry, but I'm not good at painting people," Gwynn mumbled and stepped away.

"So you did paint this. I suspected." His smile broadened. "Oh, now I must purchase it."

"Please, sir, there's no obligation—"

"No, no. It's my pleasure."

"But I told you, it's not perfect—I mean, finished."

"Is it dry to the touch?"

"Yes, but—"

"Then I'll take it." He stuck his umbrella under his arm and picked up the canvas. "I shall hang it …" He pursed his lips then shrugged. "My granddaughters-in-law will find a spot, I'm sure. My workshop's big enough." He handed her the canvas. "Wrap this up for me, will you, please?"

Chapter Two

COMPELLED BY the hint of authority in the old man's voice, Gwynn laid baking paper and bubble wrap atop the counter. "You have a workshop?" she asked, centering the painting on the paper. "What do you make?"

"Toys. My, uh, employees and I make childhood wishes come true."

Gwynn smirked. "Of course you do." Twinkling eyes. Deep laugh. White beard. He even had the "little round belly" that prevented his jacket from closing. This man probably dressed the part of Santa every year in his hometown Christmas parade. She wanted to dislike him for that reason alone but couldn't. He exuded kindness.

She drew the bubble wrap over the paper and said, "I used to know a boy who hoped to open his own workshop one day." Blue eyes that could rival Paul Newman's surfaced in her mind, but she swiped a mental hand to dispel the memory.

"Does he make toys too? Are you saying I have competition?"

Gwynn taped the wrapping at the edges and forced a smile. "I don't know that it ever happened, actually. We lost touch."

"That's too bad." He pointed to the painting. "How much do I owe you? And I won't accept anything less than a fair price."

Gwynn quoted him what she believed reasonable for a near-finished product by an amateur.

He pulled out his wallet and counted out paper bills. "I lost touch with a friend long ago," he said. "We had a falling out, you see, and we wouldn't talk to each other for years. Later, I wanted to make things right, but …" He shook his head. "It was too late."

Gwynn pressed her lips together as she slid the wrapped painting into a wide, ribbon-handled paper bag emblazoned with the gallery logo. "I'm so sorry."

"You have people you love in your life?"

Unexpected tears stung her eyes, and she cleared her throat. "Yes, sir. Some live across the country"—like her Uncle Russ and Aunt Maude Davison—"and some are beyond my earthly reach." Like Poppa Jeb and Mama Edith, the darling elderly couple who'd taken her in as a crazy teenager but who had died in a car accident two years ago.

"Ah." The man grimaced. "I apologize, child, if I opened a wound. But then, you understand what this old geezer is trying to say, don't you?"

"To appreciate my loved ones before they're gone." She held out the bag. "Thank goodness for technology and video calls."

The Santa look-alike quirked a bushy eyebrow. "You and I both know the people on the other end of those calls would prefer a physical hug to a spoken one." He took the bag and reached across the counter to squeeze her upper arm. "Don't let fear hold you prisoner, Hadley, or you'll wake up one day and realize you not only missed out on a friendship, like I did, but you missed out on *life*."

Ice flooded Gwynn's veins as he turned and shuffled to the

door. "How do you know that name?" she demanded. No one had uttered it in almost ten years.

But he exited the store as if he hadn't heard her. Outside, he snapped open his umbrella, secured the bag under his arm, turned left down the sidewalk, and disappeared from view.

Gwynn trembled.

How dare he use that name and imply she lived in fear! She had *escaped* her fears and been given a second chance at life— ensconced in safety—with Poppa Jeb and Mama Edith, thanks to the Davisons. Who was this Santa impersonator to suggest otherwise? Did he have connections to Uncle Russ or Aunt Maude in Prospect? Did he know something she didn't?

With Michael Bublé's version of "Blue Christmas" trilling through the speakers, Gwynn snatched her phone and tapped the Davisons' number on her "favorites" list. Irene could potentially explode like an uncapped smoothie machine if she caught Gwynn using her phone during business hours, but hearing a friendly voice was more important at the moment.

The phone rang three times before someone picked up.

"Are you okay, dear?" Concern laced Aunt Maude's voice on the other end.

Gwynn emitted a nervous laugh. "Hello to you too."

"I'm sorry." Aunt Maude chuckled. "But it's midday, and since you never call during a work shift, I reckoned something was wrong."

Yeah—do you happen to know why a random, jolly fat man called me Hadley? "I was, uh, gently chastised earlier for not reaching out to my loved ones more often." With her free hand, Gwynn stowed the bubble wrap and baking paper under the checkout counter. "So, how are things there? Is Uncle Russ doing okay? How's Brisket?" They had the most mischievous little Havanese with the most innocent "who, me?" puppy-dog eyes Gwynn had ever seen. Not that she'd met Brisket in person, but Aunt Maude filled their text thread with endless doggy pics.

"Oh, we're all doing fine. Russ bought Brisket a remote-controlled truck."

"*Another* one? What's that make, three?"

"One. The other two are sports cars."

Gwynn snorted. "Are you sure Uncle Russ buys them for Brisket, or for himself?"

"You've seen the videos. Brisket loves to chase them around the house."

"Uh huuuh." Gwynn drew out the syllable.

"Hmph. Russ spoils Brisket and I spoil Russ, what can I say? Other than that, we're busy getting ready for the Christmas Jamboree next weekend."

"Oh, gracious." Gwynn put a hand to her forehead. "That means I'm behind on my Christmas shopping. Are you entering the pie contest again?"

"You bet. Can't let Annabelle Richards best me for the fourth year in a row." Aunt Maude tsked. "You know she's won—"

"Seven times in the last decade, yes, I know. I haven't had your huckleberry pie in a while, but I do remember an amazing blend of tart and—"

"Oh, no!" Aunt Maude let out a strangled cry. "Russ? Oh, good heavens!"

Gwynn's hand tightened around her phone. "What is it? What's wrong?"

"Russ! It's going to be okay, honey." Commotion sounded in the background. "Gwynn, I gotta go. We need to get him to the hospital."

"But—"

The line went dead. Gwynn's mouth dropped and her heart pounded. Uncle Russ … to the hospital? What happened? Did he have a stroke? A heart attack?

I should be there.

"No, Gwynn, are you crazy?" she hissed. Circumstances in

Prospect hadn't changed. It wasn't safe for her.

Yet the words from Santa's double replayed in her mind. She'd never forgive herself if Uncle Russ was on his deathbed and she refused to see him one last time because of cowardice.

Oh, Lord, what do I do, what do I do?

"Why are you gawking at the entrance like a buffoon?"

Gwynn blinked. Irene sashayed across the floor as she peeled off her black gloves, the front door closing behind her. Gwynn's mouth snapped shut. "I'm sorry. I was … just … I was on the phone—"

"Yes, I can see that." Irene's dark eyes narrowed at the apparatus in Gwynn's hand. "I'll be docking a half hour from your wages today."

Less messy than a frenzied smoothie. "Irene, I have to go." Gwynn tossed her phone into her handbag and searched for her peacoat.

"I beg your pardon. We don't close until five."

"This is urgent." She shrugged into her coat, her thoughts whirling with the sudden change in plans. "I'll have to get the next flight out—"

"*Flight?* Where do you think you're going?"

"Montana." Gwynn shuddered. Had she seriously uttered that word? "But don't worry—I'll be back in time for the show next Saturday."

"Young lady, if you leave now, you may find yourself without a job to come back to."

Gwynn inhaled. *Lord, I need this job.* "Irene, I'm sorry, but this is an emergency. My uncle, he's … ill, and …" *Please, God, let him be okay. I can't lose him too.* "And I need to see him." Whether Gwynn liked it or not.

Apparently, God was trying to tell her something, after all.

Chapter Three

"FLIGHT ATTENDANTS, please prepare for arrival," the captain said over the plane's intercom.

Gwynn's stomach somersaulted, and her pencil stalled on her notepad where she sketched the lilies from the woman's purse beside her. As passengers in the cabin stowed away their tray tables and turned off their electronics, she glanced out the tiny oval window to her left. Thousands of feet below, the snow-laden Rocky Mountains stretched like a rippling white blanket under a rich blue sky. A dark ribbon of water wound its way through deep valleys dotted with evergreens and occasional towns. Truly a work of art by the Master Himself.

Her fingers tightened on her pencil, a desire to capture the beauty on paper warring with her inner tension.

"I'm coming out for you and Uncle Russ," she had told Aunt Maude once she'd purchased her tickets. "Nobody else. That's the plan. Promise me no one will remember a Gwynn Sadler after I'm gone."

But it didn't matter that Aunt Maude had welcomed Gwynn's impulsive trip, or that she'd convinced Irene to give her a few days off. The peace that had guided Gwynn ever since she'd decided to visit had deserted her during her layover at the Denver airport.

Did I misunderstand You, Lord? she prayed now.

No, child. It's time, came the quiet response.

Gwynn shook out her newsboy cap and settled it on her head. Time for what, exactly?

Her movements froze. *Oh, please let it not be time for you-know-what,* she thought. *I did not agree to* that.

"Did you say something?" the woman beside her asked.

Gwynn gave a sheepish grin. "Sorry—talking to myself. Bad habit."

Once the plane pulled into the gate at the Bozeman International Airport and the seat belt sign switched off, passengers sitting beside the aisle stood to collect their things from the bins overhead. Gwynn retrieved her backpack purse from underneath the seat in front of her, slipped her sketchpad into the main pocket, then withdrew her phone from the side pocket. She took it off airplane mode. It chimed with a text from Holly and a voicemail from Aunt Maude.

Txt me when u arrive in Bozeman, Holly wrote, **so I know you made it safely.**

As the line in the aisle began to move, Gwynn stood, her heart beating an erratic tempo. She put a hand to her chest.

The woman with the lily purse eyed her. "Are you feeling all right?"

"Yeah." Gwynn took a deep breath. "Just never thought I'd willingly return to Montana, that's all."

"Willingly?" the woman pressed.

Gwynn lifted her shoulders in a wordless shrug and dropped her gaze to her phone. A stranger didn't need her sob story.

Made it, she texted Holly. **You haven't killed my goldfish,**

have you? Gwynn would have preferred a dog, but their apartment didn't allow four-legged pets.

While waiting for a response, she buttoned her peacoat—a splurge from Quincy Market because of its rich plum hue—and tapped into her voicemail. Her gaze drifted out the window again to the workers unloading suitcases from the plane's belly.

"Hello, Gwynn dear," Aunt Maude said. "I can't wait to see you." Her voice sounded joyful. Did that mean Uncle Russ was home from the hospital? She still didn't know what had happened, since Aunt Maude evaded her questions with meaningless doggy commentary. "I'm afraid, however, that our car won't start, so I won't be able to pick you up at the airport."

Gwynn frowned. If not Aunt Maude, then who—

"But I made a few calls," her aunt continued, "and learned that Cash Cooper is in Bozeman today for business. He's agreed to give you a ride and will meet you at Baggage Claim."

Gwynn's stomach pitched like a suitcase tossed onto the conveyor belt. This was *not* part of the plan!

"I know it's not ideal," Aunt Maude hastened on, as if she'd anticipated Gwynn's reaction, "but I don't have a better option. I'm so sorry. I'll be praying for you, sweetheart. You pray too. See you soon."

You pray too.

Seriously? Pray for what? Of all the people in Prospect Aunt Maude could have reached out to, she chose *Cash Cooper*? Would he recognize her? Years had passed. She'd dyed her hair, wore colored contacts, she was no longer an awkward teenager … and he thought she was dead.

Would that be enough to conceal her identity?

It had to be.

Lord, what are You doing? Gwynn shoved the phone into her backpack and eased into the aisle. *I agreed to visit the Davisons,* she argued, yanking her carry-on from the overhead bin and extending its handle with a jerk. *Nothing more.* She huffed and tugged her peacoat back into place. *I call foul, Lord.*

Probably not what Aunt Maude had in mind when she'd suggested Gwynn pray.

Holly called as Gwynn exited the plane and followed signs for Baggage Claim.

"Heya!" Holly sang. "Not to boast, but I make a fantastic pet-sitter. Your fish are having quite the party right now, belly dancing at the top of the tank."

Gwynn let out a weak laugh. "Funny."

"Well, *I* thought so. You okay?"

"Aunt Maude can't pick me up, so she sent someone else to do it."

"You make it sound like Armageddon is upon us."

"It's a fifty-minute drive from the airport to Prospect," Gwynn groused, maneuvering her carry-on to descend the escalator. A type-A businessman jockeyed past in his rush to who-knew-where.

"So, you have to spend fifty minutes with a stranger. Small talk never stumped you before."

"Precisely. Before *now.*"

Holly fell silent, and Gwynn imagined her twirling a lock of her russet hair. "I don't get it," Holly finally said. "Is she not a stranger?"

"*He.*"

Holly let out a chirp of excitement. "All the better—and potentially cozier. Is he young? Single?"

"Holly!" Gwynn laughed. At the base of the escalator, she moved with the crowd to Baggage Claim where a sculpted bronze grizzly bear sat on a podium and welcomed the tourists. "I barely glance at the guys back east. What makes you think a Stetson-toting ranch hand will catch my—"

Someone bumped into her from behind, knocking her phone

to the floor and sending her stumbling into a broad torso. Strong hands cupped her elbows and steadied her. "Hey!" she said, glaring after the offender.

A white-haired fellow wearing a red plaid jacket hurried away between passengers. The Santa look-alike from Gilded Editions! He lifted a hand in … what, a wave of apology? An acknowledgment of his bad manners? Gwynn frowned. Had he been on her flight? What were the odds—

"Are you all right, ma'am?"

The smooth baritone slipped over her collar on a delicious shiver, and her attention snapped to the man who had steadied her. Who now stooped to pick up her phone. A black Stetson shielded his face.

Her heart pounded. Was it him?

Holly's tinny, hysterical voice emitted through the phone's speaker, and the man straightened with a chuckle. "Good news— it's not broken." He raised his head as he handed the phone to Gwynn. Pale blue eyes pierced her from beneath his hat brim.

Eyes that could rival Paul Newman's.

Sweet jumpin' Jehoshaphat. She sucked in much-needed air. "Thank you," she whispered. "I'm sure I'm fine. I mean, *it's* fine. We're both fine. I mean—" Gwynn coughed, heat racing into her face. Hang those blue eyes. She brought the phone to her ear. "Holly? I'm gonna call you back." Stashing the phone in her backpack, she gave the man—*him*—Cash freakin' Cooper—a tight-lipped smile. "Sorry for bumping into you." *Lord, please, don't let him recognize me.*

His mouth crooked at the corner, his jawline blurred by dark scruff. "Can't say I've ever seen an old man charge like a bull through a crowd, but I'm happy to be your impromptu guardrail." He gave her a quick once-over, and an electric current shimmied down her spine. Then his eyebrows pulled together.

Uh oh, here it comes. Gwynn tightened her grip on her backpack straps and zipped another prayer toward Heaven.

"Are you Gwynn Sadler?"

She blinked. "Huh?" Not the name she expected.

With another chuckle, he reached behind him and pulled out a piece of paper folded like an accordion. He snapped it open. Large black letters spelled out, *Gwynn Sadler.* "I'm here to pick up a woman I haven't met and hoped I wouldn't need this. You match the description I was given, so I thought maybe—"

"Oh. Right. No. I mean, yes. I—" She relaxed her grip and forced a laugh. *Thank you, Lord, for shielding his vision!* "That's me. I'm Gwynn Sadler."

His grin widened. "Okay, then." He refolded the sign and shoved it in his back pocket before touching his hat brim in greeting. "Cash Cooper. Did Miss Maude tell you I'm your ride to Prospect?"

"She did. Nice to … meet you." *Again. As an adult.* After years avoiding thoughts of this man, Gwynn allowed herself a brief, surreptitious appraisal, her gaze traveling from his Stetson and the dark hair curling under its brim, to the brown Carhartt jacket he wore over a burnt orange, plaid flannel shirt, to his faded jeans and dusty cowboy boots. His shoulders had broadened from the lanky teenager of her youth, and the lay of his clothes hinted at more muscles than she remembered.

And from what she glimpsed of his hands, he bore no wedding ring.

Her gaze returned to his face, colliding with the interest mirrored in his eyes. Perhaps she'd been a touch premature in what she'd told Holly on the phone. Goodbye, city boys. Hello, Cash Cooper—

He's not part of the plan! her mind screeched.

Gwynn broke eye contact. Right. The plan. She adjusted her newsboy cap then clutched her backpack straps again as if they could anchor her to reality. "So, um …"

"Yeah." Cash rubbed his ear and gestured toward the baggage carousel. "Do you need to grab any bags, or are you good to go?"

She patted the handle to her carry-on. "All set."

"Excellent." He moved toward an exit, inclining his head for her to follow. "I'm parked out this way."

They emerged from the airport into a feisty, biting wind that batted at her cap and tangled her hair and scarf. She huddled into her peacoat, head down as she followed Cash across the parking lot. When he stopped beside a black Ford truck, she looked up. A sigh escaped.

Beneath a big blue dome streaked with feathery clouds stood layers of mountains marbled with evergreens and snow. They loomed behind the airport and spread out on each side, jabbing the sky with their ragged edges and tapering to a distant range in the west.

"I could sit here for hours with canvas and paint and not get bored," Gwynn said as Cash took her carry-on and slid it along the backseat.

"One would think you'd never seen mountains before," he teased.

Oh, but it had been so long. "You're familiar with them, so their splendor is lost on you. For me, in Boston, the only mountains on my horizon are made of brick and steel." Gwynn slipped her backpack purse from her shoulders and turned to find him studying her, a small line between his brows. Her smile faltered. "Did I say something wrong?"

"Hmm?" Cash straightened. "No, ma'am." Stepping aside, he opened the passenger door for her.

Gwynn's eyebrows rose. "A gentleman." Still. Grabbing the inside handle, she hopped onto the seat. "I feared they'd gone extinct."

"Not all of us. You just gotta know where to look." Cash winked with a lopsided grin before shutting her door. A grin that made her insides go squirrelly.

Lord, have mercy on me. Gwynn wedged her bag by her feet as he rounded the truck to the driver's side. *I'm returning to Boston in a few days, and okay, sure, You did fiiiine work when fashioning Cash, but You know he's not my type.*

Not anymore.

Cash eased behind the wheel and started the engine. "Let's get you home to Miss Maude, shall we?"

Chapter Four

HOME.

The word rattled inside Gwynn's head as they turned off Interstate 90 onto a local highway that wove through the Bridger Mountains. The steep rock faces rolled past her window, one after another.

Had she ever considered any place home? Technically, not even Poppa Jeb and Mama Edith's farmhouse had been "home." And the one place that could have claimed the label she'd rather not recall.

Gwynn shuddered and hugged her arms.

"Cold?" Cash turned the temperature dial on his dash.

She smiled. "Thanks."

"Remind me again of your relation to the Davisons." Cash glanced at his rearview window, then at her. He'd removed his hat, and loose chestnut curls fell over his forehead. Why did guys always get the to-die-for hair? "I believe Miss Maude told me you're her niece? Have you ever been out to visit?"

His question may have implied "been here before," but she latched onto his actual words. "Visit? No." She hadn't come back since she'd fled. "And I'm more like Maude's great-niece. Uncle Russ and Mama Edith were siblings."

"And this Mama Edith is your …?"

"Grandmother." Of a sort. Before he could ask about her parents, Gwynn angled toward him and said, "Please fill me in on the latest with Uncle Russ."

"The latest?"

"Yeah. Has he been released from the hospital yet? Aunt Maude won't tell me anything about his condition, but I was on the phone with her when it happened."

Cash frowned. "When what happened, exactly?"

"That's what I'm trying to figure out. We were having a normal conversation when she started exclaiming and saying Uncle Russ needed to get to the hospital."

"Russ? Oh!" Cash let out a half-laugh. "No, you misunderstood. Miss Maude didn't take *Russ* to the hospital. They took their *dog* to the hospital. The *Wonderfur Animal Hospital*. Seems Brisket had a seizure."

"What?" Gwynn's heart bungee-jumped behind her ribcage. "You mean, Uncle Russ is okay?"

"Russ is as healthy as anyone half his age."

"He's not dying?"

"Nope."

"You're sure?"

Cash grinned. "Positive."

Gwynn exhaled on a whoosh and slumped against the seat. "What a relief. I've been wallowing in guilt for not having visited sooner, even though—" She shook her head, letting the sentence drop. Then she straightened again. "But that means I came here under false pretenses, and my job is on the line because I left with barely a warning." Whisking off her cap, she told him of the terse exchange with Irene, adding, "Why would Aunt Maude lie to me? Why would she lead me to think Uncle Russ was on his death-bed?"

"You're sure she knew you thought *Russ* was at the hospital?"

"Hundred percent." Gwynn fidgeted with the brim of her cap. "It's not like her to deceive me." *But it's a concept you're all too familiar with,* she chided herself, *so who are you to judge?*

The childhood scar on her left hand peeped out from her coat sleeve. Was it a trick of the light or did it glow neon red? She glanced at Cash and tugged her sleeve lower to hide the scar.

Who was she to judge, indeed?

Settling back into her seat, Gwynn pressed her temple against the windowpane with a conflicted sigh.

"Can you change your flight?" Cash asked.

A narrow valley blanketed in snow unfurled around them, heads of cattle meandering in the distance. "I used a small airline—cheaper that way—and they only fly on Mondays and Thursdays. I'm stuck for the next few days."

"So, make the most of your visit. Especially now that you know Russ is fine."

She smiled out the window. "I'll certainly enjoy these Montana views." She had adjusted to city life, but the broad valleys and majestic mountains reignited something dormant within her. For several quiet moments, she soaked up their splendor.

Eventually, however, she couldn't ignore the probing glances Cash tossed her way as he navigated the winding road. She peeked at him from the corner of her eye. "It's rude to stare, you know," she said, keeping her voice light. "What happened to the gentle-man from the airport?"

"Sorry." He spliced a hand through his hair, the brown locks flopping back over his forehead. "You remind me of someone, but for the life of me, I can't remember who."

Heat crept up her torso, and she loosened her scarf. *Keep him blind, Lord.*

"Plus, you seemed … hungry a moment ago, peering out the window."

"Ah. Well." Gwynn emitted a soft laugh. "I *am* an artist. And this landscape is beyond inspirational. Just imagine these mountains and evergreens painted as a mural on a living room wall. Or a field of wildflowers dancing above a baby's crib on a frameless canvas, their petals dappled from a late spring snowfall. Add a whimsical touch for a child's playroom. For so long, I—" She squelched her thoughts. A mere twenty minutes in the truck with Cash had her running at the mouth. What did that mean for her over the next three days? "For so long, I listened to Aunt Maude gush about Montana's beauty, and now, here I am," she finished.

"Here you are." He ran a hand over the scruff on his jaw, his gaze moving between her and the road. "You mentioned Boston earlier. Is that where you live? You've done well if you can afford Boston prices on an artist's salary."

"Oh, I'm only an artist when I'm not adulting. To afford Boston, I work in an art gallery, dine on ramen noodles, and share an apartment with two suite mates. Mia is an accountant with long office hours. The other, Holly, is my best friend from college and a fellow starving artist. She was the one I was talking to when I got bulldozed—oh! Hang on a sec." Gwynn reached into her backpack, withdrew her phone, and texted Holly she was okay and would call her later. She sent Cash a rueful smile as she tucked the phone away again. "Sorry. I try not to text in the middle of a conversation, but I did end my chat with Hols rather abruptly."

"Fair point." Cash inclined his head. "As a 'starving artist,' does she also paint?"

"No, she throws. As in pottery. She makes amazing dinnerware … and brings new meaning to the Bible verse that says we are the clay and the Lord is our potter." Gwynn plucked a piece of fuzz from her cap. "You should see her frustration with stubborn, hardened clay."

"Hence why we should stay moldable."

"Yeeess." She propped her elbow on the window frame. "Tell me I'm not the only one who finds that concept challenging."

"You're not the only one who finds that concept challenging." His eyes crinkled as he glanced at her. "Are you a believer, then?"

Gwynn nodded.

Cash inclined his head. "Me too. Though I've veered off course at times."

"Don't we all?"

They shared a grin, a measure of understanding and friendliness in his gaze, and her pulse kicked at the full impact of his blue eyes. A memory flashed from another time. Another truck. Another conversation drawing two lovestruck teenagers closer together. An ache burned in her throat, and she looked away. *Pull it together, Sadler!*

"So, what about you?" she asked once the threat of tears subsided. "What do you do? Aunt Maude said you had business that took you into Bozeman."

"Yeah, I'm seeking another vendor to sell my work. Not many options for that in li'l ol' Prospect."

"Are you an artist too?"

"Not in the typical sense. I'm a carpenter. Power tools are my canvas."

"Carpentry." Gwynn's mouth lifted at the corners. Had he seen his dream to fruition, then? *It suits him.*

"It does? How so?"

Oh, heavens, she'd said that out loud? She squirmed and pulled the scarf fully from around her neck. "I-I just mean, you look like a guy who's comfortable with power tools. An all-around handyman." Gwynn's eyes flared. "Don't take that the wrong way. I'm sure you'd rock a business suit, but tool belts are hot—" *Oh. My. Word!* She hid her face in her scarf, her cheeks flaming. "Ignore me. I'm alone in the art gallery most days, and I've formed this annoying habit of talking out loud."

Cash chuckled. "Annoying to you, perhaps. Helpful for me."

She lowered her hands. A grin lingered on his lips, and she cocked an eyebrow. "Helpful?"

"A man can learn a lot from a woman's inner thoughts."

She swallowed. He could learn too much if she didn't check herself.

Chapter Five

GWYNN'S INSIDES had coiled tighter than a used-up tube of paint by the time the truck crossed inside Prospect's borders. How could Aunt Maude have tricked her into coming?

How could God have allowed it?

It's time.

There came those words again, as clearly as if God physically sat in the truck. Fear battled with peace, and she took a deep breath.

"You okay?" Cash asked, turning onto a wide road flanked by buildings in the typical western false front architecture.

"Mmm-hmm." Gwynn rolled her shoulders. "Long day of travel." Late afternoon shadows stretched across the street as the sun descended toward the mountainous horizon.

"Hang in there for a few more minutes. This is Broadway, our main street that runs north and south for several blocks."

She nodded and affected the role of a first-time visitor.

Cash braked to allow a family to cross the road, raising a finger to them in greeting. "Here you'll find your common shops like the grocer's and bookstores, novelty shops like Tony's Glassworks, vacant buildings harkening back to a more prosperous time, and"—he pointed down the street with a lopsided grin—"the only traffic light in town."

As he resumed speed, Gwynn craned her neck to read the storefront names. Several had changed in the last decade; some remained the same. Christmas lights and garland wound along lampposts and zig-zagged overhead. "Do you have a shop for your carpentry business?"

"Yes, although I technically co-own it with my mentor. He's hoping I buy him out soon, but contrary to what my name might imply, I'm tight on funds."

"I know that feeling. Who's your mentor?"

"Gramps. Frank Holliday when you first meet him, but after that, everyone calls him Gramps."

"Gramps," Gwynn whispered, fingers splayed on the window. "Sounds like a much-loved man." Memories pressed against the cage in her mind, but she avoided it, focusing instead on sounding like a newcomer. "And is your shop on Broadway, or elsewhere?"

Cash indicated a two-storied green barn with white trim up ahead that looked out of place among the blockier structures. Above the barn doors hung a rustic, hand-hewn sign displaying the words, *Plane & Knotty Carpentry*. Below the sign, a black wooden arrow pointed to a door that had been cut into the larger barn door—with a child-sized door cut into the adult-sized door.

So, Gramps still catered to a child's fancy.

"I love it," Gwynn said. "What do you make? Furniture? Toys? Cabinetry?"

"You'll have to swing by and see for yourself." Cash gave her a slow grin. "I'll make sure to wear my tool belt."

She groaned but couldn't suppress a smile of her own. "You're not going to let that drop, are you?"

"Not unless you give me reason to."

Gwynn studied his profile, the hard planes of his face, the straight slope of his nose, his perfectly mussed curls begging for a finger-comb. Easy on the eyes coupled with chivalry to melt the heart. She had a hundred good reasons not to encourage him—for both their sakes—but she couldn't voice a single one.

He passed under the green light and drove for another two blocks before turning down a side street. "Almost there."

They went one more block, turned onto yet another street, and passed three houses before pulling to a stop in front of a two-story house with smoke blue siding. Vintage candles flickered in each window, and the shades were drawn halfway in the upper two dormers. Garland and white Christmas lights swathed the front porch and underlined the windows, and an evergreen wreath with an oversize red bow graced the paneled door.

"It's like something you'd see on a vintage Christmas card," Gwynn whispered.

Here she'd be able to fully relax with the two people in Prospect who knew her worst secrets and loved her anyway.

She reached for the door handle, but Cash touched her arm. "That's my job, remember?"

Gwynn cocked an eyebrow again.

"It's not a reflection of your capabilities, Gwynn, but a show of respect on my part … and maybe a touch of reverence."

"Reverence?"

His lips lifted. "Yes, ma'am. The female sex baffles us men."

"I take it 'ma'am' is considered another show of respect?"

"Uh, yes … ma'am."

She pursed her lips to hide a grin. "Except, it makes me feel old, and you're older than I am."

"How do you figure that?" With mock offense, Cash pulled down the visor to check his reflection in the mirror. "Do I look old?"

Gwynn laughed. "You look perfect."

Cash shot her a sly smile. "Perfect, huh?"

Her cheeks warmed. "I mean fine. You look fine."

"You said perfect."

Too perfect for her. She tugged her newsboy cap into place. "Will you please open my door, now?"

"I don't know. From where I sit, the longer you talk, the better I sound."

"You're a flirt."

"Guilty as charged." He reached into the backseat for his Stetson and settled it atop his head. His striking eyes regarded her from beneath the brim. "And it's completely uncharacteristic of me."

Gwynn snorted. "Right."

"I promise." Cash slowly drew back his door handle. "Have you ever met a person you immediately clicked with and felt like you'd known them forever?"

Her heart thumped. "Yes."

"Yeah." He stared at her a moment longer, wrapping her in crystal blue warmth, then shook his head and hopped from the cab.

Gwynn blew out her breath, looped her scarf about her neck, and once again tugged her coat sleeve over her scar. *Okay, Lord, You've made Your point*, she prayed as Cash walked around the truck. *I still find him attractive. Will You lay off now? I have a plan, and You're supposed to help me stick to it.*

Even though her plan had already altered with the good news about Uncle Russ.

Her door opened and Cash stepped aside, offering his gloved hand. "Careful when you step out. There's black ice."

More chivalry? "Thanks." Taking his hand, she moved from truck to sidewalk—and promptly lost traction.

Cash seized her waist to keep her upright, and the action hauled her against him. She inhaled a mix of spice and wood shavings. Her body hummed as heat enveloped her despite the frigid mountain air.

"That's the second time today you've saved me from kissing the ground."

Interest flared in his eyes. "My pleasure."

"N-not kissing," she murmured. "Wrong word."

"Freudian slip?" He gave a lazy smile, his gaze roaming her face. Slowly, his eyebrows drew together, and the interest in his eyes retreated behind shutters of wariness. Cash set her away from him, gripping her upper arms. "*Hadley?*"

She froze. "What?"

"You're Hadley Jacobs." Cash's hands tightened. "And yet, you can't be. Your eyes and hair color are wrong. And she's—"

"Gwynn, you made it!"

The excited cry came from the house, and Gwynn broke from Cash's hold as Aunt Maude shuffled down the porch stairs, throwing a winter coat over an ivory sweater. "I'm so sorry about the icy patches. I saw you slip. Are you all right?"

On shaky limbs, Gwynn met the tiny woman on the path halfway to the house and received the frail but heartfelt embrace, tears leaking from her eyes. "I should be livid with you," she said, "but it's good to see you."

"Oh, sweetie." Aunt Maude drew back and cupped Gwynn's face. "I'm sorry I wasn't honest about Russ. He's inside with Brisket, putting the kettle on for tea. He can't wait to see you." She smiled past Gwynn. "Cash, honey, thank you for bringing her home. You want to take those inside?"

Gwynn turned as Cash set her carry-on and backpack purse on the sidewalk.

"I made huckleberry pie," Aunt Maude added. "Have a slice before leaving."

Cash removed his hat and drilled a hand through his hair. "Mind if I take a rain check?" He glanced at Gwynn, his eyes weighted with unspoken questions.

If he expected answers, he'd have to ask elsewhere.

"No pressure to stay. You're still a gentleman in my book"—with an easy smile, Gwynn stepped forward to grab her things—"even if you don't bring these inside." She didn't blame him for running. She'd run, too, if she'd seen a ghost from the past.

His posture relaxed. "It was nice meeting you … Gwynn."

"You too."

He opened his mouth as though to say more, then closed it again and gave a slight tug on the brim of his Stetson. Nodding to Aunt Maude, he walked around his truck and hopped inside the cab.

"I suppose it was too much to hope that he would stay a little longer," Aunt Maude said as the truck rumbled to life and moved away from the curb. "You know, it was the darnedest thing. About thirty minutes ago, Russ came out to try starting the car one more time before calling a tow truck, and it started right up!"

"Hmm." Gwynn pursed her lips and extended her carry-on handle. "You sure this dysfunctional car wasn't a ruse to throw Cash and me together?"

Aunt Maude held up three fingers. "Scout's honor." Then she wagged her eyebrows. "I saw him catch you when you slipped, though. You two looked good—"

"No matchmaking, Aunt Maude. It's bad enough you made me think Uncle Russ was dying."

"Tut tut." The woman waved her off and trudged toward the porch. At the end of the block, Cash's truck turned the corner and disappeared.

Out of sight, Gwynn mused, following Aunt Maude into the house. *But how long before I can put Cash Cooper out of my mind … for the second time?*

Chapter Six

IF THE exterior of the Davisons' house looked like a Christmas card, the interior looked like a kitschy Christmas shop. Decorations covered every horizontal surface from snow globes to plush snowmen to reindeer figurines to three different sets of Dept 56 villages. Pre-lit garland swathed the staircase banister in the central hallway and draped the fireplace mantel in the living room. Three four-foot evergreen trees stood at attention alongside the staircase in the hallway, and a six-foot tree held prominence by the living room windows. There was even a *Christmas Story* lamp in the dining room.

The Grinch would be horrified.

And if Gwynn, currently seated at the dining table, turned her head just so, she could peer through the doorway, across the central hall, and into the living room to look the worst offender in his jolly glass eyes.

Aunt Maude's very own, three-foot Santa Claus.

Contrary to Irene's Santa at the art gallery sporting its classic red suit and black belt, this one wore Old World garb. A sack of wrapped boxes lay at its feet where it guarded the main Christmas tree.

He knows if you've been bad or good …

A memory leaked from its cage and floated to the floor of her mind. Like most children, Gwynn had stopped believing in Santa sometime before the third grade. But Frank Holliday—the one-and-only Gramps—had kept the fun alive with his own "Letters to Santa" mailbox, encouraging the kids in town to drop off their letters year-round and he'd make sure Santa received them.

Gwynn had later discovered Gramps read the letters himself and tried to fulfill as many Christmas wishes as he could. For kicks, she had slipped a few letters into the mailbox even as an older child, asking for a new sled or a new pair of mittens after hers had become thin and ratty, and he'd never let her down.

Then came the year everything blew up in her face—

"Here we go!"

From the kitchen, Aunt Maude backed her way through the adjoining swinging door, huckleberry pie in hand. At her heels, Brisket scooted into the dining room, appearing for all the world like a normal, healthy dog that hadn't suffered a seizure the other day.

Gwynn straightened in her chair as Aunt Maude set the pie on the table. "That looks fantastic."

"Let's pray it tastes fantastic." Aunt Maude turned to the sideboard bedecked with a Dickens' Christmas village and tsked at her husband who rummaged in the bottom drawer. "Russell Davison, what are you doing down there?" she asked. She opened a top drawer and removed a serrated pie server.

"I'm trying to find … this." With a wide grin, Uncle Russ held up an album and pushed to his feet, Brisket jumping and pawing at his leg. "Here, sweetheart." He slid the album on the table toward Gwynn. "You'll get a kick out of this."

As he took a seat across the table and lifted Brisket onto his lap, Gwynn opened the album cover. A laugh escaped at the baby photo she recognized. "Is this whole album of me?" She flipped through several pages of glossy pictures taken during her middle school days, the layouts embellished with stickers, washi tape, and scrapbook frames. Yellowed newspaper clippings and a few worn photographs highlighted big moments from her early years.

She turned another page, and her breath hitched at the photo centered there, four round faces smiling out at her. Two siblings, Uncle Russ and Mama Edith, with their two spouses, Aunt Maude and Poppa Jeb. When Poppa and Mama had gone to be with their Savior a few years ago, the pang in Gwynn's heart proved that one needn't be blood relatives to feel the exquisite pain caused by a loved one's earthly absence.

"Where would I be without you four brave souls?" Gwynn whispered, smiling through blurry vision. She smoothed a finger over their photographed faces. Aunt Maude paused in cutting the pie and reached out to pat her hand.

Swiping at a wayward tear, Gwynn flipped another page, and a chuckle escaped. "My surprise eighteenth birthday party." Poppa Jeb had captured the shock on her face for all time. "I forgot you two came."

"Edith had been so proud that she'd managed to keep the celebration and our visit a secret," Aunt Maude said, transferring slices of pie onto three porcelain dessert plates.

"And then you attempted to outdo her homemade birthday cake the next day."

Aunt Maude wrinkled her nose as she set a plate in front of Gwynn. "I do have a competitive streak, don't I? Along those lines"—she handed out forks and fresh napkins—"you two shall be my guinea pigs since Cash insisted on a rain check."

"Gladly." Uncle Russ pulled his plate closer even as he readjusted Brisket to keep the dog from licking his food.

"Guinea pigs?" Gwynn sunk her fork into the crust, which flaked apart. "You've made huckleberry pies before."

"I tweaked the recipe for the upcoming Christmas Jamboree." Aunt Maude took a seat beside Uncle Russ and draped a napkin on her lap. "I told you about Annabelle Richards the other day. I am determined to win this year."

Gwynn scooped up a wedge of pie. "You're a feisty old lady."

"Yes, well, I've earned that right after all these decades." She twirled her fork in the air. "This will be the most rewarding Jamboree ever."

For Aunt Maude, maybe. For Gwynn, her most rewarding Jam was the year she'd received her first official kiss from her crush behind a darkened kiosk as the snowflakes fell about them.

Ugh, you're not supposed to go there, she rebuked herself.

Giving a tiny shake of her head, she brought the pie to her mouth. The tangy sweetness of the huckleberries hit her tongue, and she closed her eyes on a contented moan. "Delicious. If you don't win, I'm gonna suspect Mrs. Richards of bribing the judges. What did you change?"

Brisket stretched over Uncle Russ's lap and sniffed at the crust and berry filling stacked on Aunt Maude's fork. She pushed his nose away. "I went heavy on the cinnamon and was *very* generous with the butter."

"In other words, you're going to give Uncle Russ an actual heart attack." When she'd greeted him earlier, Gwynn had joked that nothing harmful could ever befall him before clearing it with her first.

The older woman's eyes crinkled. "Then we must give Cash an ample portion of this pie, so Russ doesn't eat too much himself. You can take it to him tomorrow." Gwynn began to protest, but Aunt Maude barreled on. "Enough small talk. We endured it through dinner. I want to know how you're *really* doing."

"But I already told you—"

"No." She pointed her fork at Gwynn. "I want the skinny on romance. Are you still dating those Business Suits?"

"Aunt Maude!" Gwynn laughed. "You *are* feisty."

"That's what Russ calls your beaus. He met one the last time he visited. Do you recall when I sprained my ankle and couldn't come?"

"That would have been"—Gwynn squinted at the ceiling—"Quinton Baker. He was ... nice. Needed table manners."

"And then there was Isaac. Followed by Mike. And ..." Aunt Maude nudged Uncle Russ with her elbow. "Wasn't there another Suit?"

"Logan," Uncle Russ said.

"Don't ever let anyone tell you your minds are going," Gwynn grumbled. "Yes, Logan asked me out to dinner, but he made it clear we were going Dutch. He was nice too. They were all nice, I suppose. Nice to look at. Nice to talk to." She popped another piece of pie in her mouth. After swallowing, she added, "Their values weren't always nice, though. Most didn't align with mine. Even guys I've met at church have questionable morals." With a sigh, she pushed a few huckleberries around the edge of her plate, the sauce smearing across the blue and white print. "I think I'm broken."

"Oh, honey, society's broken, not you."

"Though you don't do yourself any favors by dating the wrong kind of guy," Uncle Russ said in a gruff tone, scratching Brisket under his chin. The dog's eyes drifted closed.

"And what kind of guy would you suggest I date?"

"Well ... Cash is single." Aunt Maude smiled. "Now there's a gentleman with a bit of an edge. He'd challenge you. Go head-to-head with you, get you all fired up, invigorate your soul."

Gwynn exchanged a glance with Uncle Russ. "Sounds more like an adversary than a boyfriend."

"And you two already have chemistry."

"Aunt Maude—"

"I'm talking about earlier today. I saw those sparks flying."

"Then did you notice when I scared him off with my face?" Gwynn hiked her eyebrows at the elderly couple. "Seems I remind him of *someone* he knows. Besides, he's not part of my plan while I'm here."

"Probably better that way," Uncle Russ said around a forkful of pie. "Tessa Reynolds has her sights on him."

Gwynn's tummy squirmed. "Tessa's still around?"

"And her daddy's still a pastor."

She worried her bottom lip.

Uncle Russ scooped up berries with the side of his fork. "It's only a matter of time before Cash relents to her dogged pursuit. That boy's not made of stone."

Aunt Maude glared at Uncle Russ. "Tessa hasn't nabbed him yet. And those two don't have sparks!"

"A relationship needs more than sparks, Aunt Maude, if it's going to last."

"It's the spark that sets the flame a'goin'," the woman countered.

"She's a *pastor's daughter.* What guy would regret choosing such a woman for—" Gwynn's mouth snapped shut as Aunt Maude's glared turned in her direction.

"You know as well as I do that pastors' children aren't safe from the devil's claws."

Gwynn held up her hands in surrender.

"Now, take you and Cash—"

"There is no me and Cash. He's not part of my plan."

"Plan-schman." Aunt Maude jabbed the table with a finger. "Did you ever submit your plan for God's approval?"

Gwynn lowered her eyes to stare at her now-empty plate and its familiar pattern of delicate trees and rounded mountains. "I was clear with you on the phone—"

An image slashed across her vision of a similar plate exploding from where it hung on the wall. Gwynn gasped, and the image vanished, taking with it all the air in the room. Leaning her elbows on the table, she covered her face with shaky hands.

"Gwynn, honey, what is it?" Uncle Russ asked.

A queasiness started in her stomach, and she squelched her mind from going down Memory Lane. That lane was—would always be—forbidden. *I didn't ask for this, Lord. I won't be a willing participant.*

"Sweetheart, are you okay?" Aunt Maude dropped into the chair beside her and rubbed her back. "I shouldn't have pushed you. At times, I'm like a pit bull on a slab of steak—"

"It's the Imari Garden plate," Gwynn whispered. "My mom used to collect them."

"Oh, shoot." Something rasped along the tablecloth. "Russ, you take this. Gwynn, I'm so sorry. I didn't think."

Gwynn shook her head and sat up, forcing a smile. "It's all right. I'll be fine."

A significant look passed between Uncle Russ and Aunt Maude.

Gwynn stiffened. "No. I know what you're going to say, and the answer is no."

Aunt Maude flattened a wrinkle in the tablecloth. "But perhaps it's time for healing."

"I *am* healed. By the blood of Jesus Christ. He changed me inside and out, and I'll be forever grateful."

"This needs closure," Uncle Russ said.

She sighed and scrubbed her hands over her face. "Some things never get closure. Some things just *are* until God metes out judgment in the end."

"Gwynn."

She met Uncle Russ's gaze, and her heart tripped at the sheen in his eyes.

"Give it some thought, huh?" he asked.

Her throat burned. She couldn't outright deny the man who had sacrificed so much for her. "Okay."

But it didn't matter how long she spent thinking. She'd arrived in Montana armed with a plan. A safe, wise plan. She wouldn't—couldn't—waver from it.

Chapter Seven

GWYNN JERKED upright, sucking in air, her heart pounding while the screams echoed inside her head. She blinked in the darkened room. Moonlight arced in a funny path across the ceiling above her.

"A dream." Her shoulders sagged, and she rubbed her temples. "Just a dream." Then why did the moonlight come from an odd angle?

"Because you're sleeping in a guest room, silly," she answered herself. Two thousand miles from her carefully crafted life. She peered at the alarm clock beside the bed. Four-thirty. Six-thirty Boston time. Time to get up, if she were there. Time to stay in bed since she was here.

Gwynn curled onto her side and shut her eyes, but the screams from her nightmare hounded her. Panic-laced death screams that had ripped through the evening air amid a hazy backdrop and faceless people in a dream she hadn't had in years.

She grimaced and tossed back the covers. Fine. She'd clear her thoughts with an early morning jog.

Rifling through her luggage, she collected her running clothes. Ten minutes later, wearing a hat, mittens, and carrying a flashlight, she ventured out into the dark, frosty morning.

She nearly turned around again after a few hundred feet.

Gwynn's body might have been awake, geared for her daily run, but she'd forgotten the side effects of high-altitude exercise. Her lungs shrieked inside her chest, and her legs moved like blocks of granite as she traversed the snow-encrusted sidewalks. And she'd only gone half a mile!

Yielding to a slow jog, she forced her attention from her body's agony to the surrounding neighborhood. Moonlight trickled down rooftops and pooled along front yards. Some houses had been lovingly tended over the years; others wilted on their foundations. A few original log cabins rotted away, relics from Prospect's booming days during the gold rush in the 1860s.

Though ranching families had moved in to replace the miners moving on, the town's population had been declining long before she'd escaped. Big cities drew away the younger generations for education, and few returned to their roots. If the trend kept up, Prospect could become a future ghost town.

Yet, if one had a past like hers, Gwynn didn't begrudge their leaving.

With her flashlight beam lighting the way, she followed the sidewalk that looped through Bentley Park.

Wrong choice. Memories clawed at their confines as she passed a water fountain, the statue of Prospect's founder, the gazebo where—

What was that?

Movement tickled in her peripheral vision, and she whipped her beam over frost-coated swings, a slide, and a jungle gym. The hair at the back of her neck prickled. Had she seen animal … or man?

A dog barked in the distance, and she licked her lips. Was someone watching her?

She carried the beam beyond the playground to a copse of evergreens, and it caught on a massive form. Her hand trembled. Thick, majestic antlers branched out atop the intelligent face of … a reindeer. It blinked, chuffed, and lowered its head, its gaze fixed on her.

The blood rushed in her ears. She got the feeling it was sizing her up.

Another bark ripped through the silence, this time closer and followed by a whistle. The reindeer snorted then spun and dashed off as two giant paws landed on Gwynn's chest. She shrieked, sprawling backward onto the ground. Adrenaline geared up for flight mode until something rough and wet slimed her chin.

Her shriek turned into a laugh, and the tension drained from her shoulders as she gave the Golden Retriever a hearty scratch behind the ears. "You scared the color right out of me." She sat up, angling her face to ward off the dog's excited kisses. "Where's your master, hmm?"

"Sawyer, heel!" Hurried footsteps crunched through old snow, and a beam of light settled over her and the dog. "I'm so sor—*Gwynn?*"

The light shone in her face, and she lifted a hand to block it, her mirth fading to caution at the familiar voice. "Good morning, Cash." What kind of reaction would she receive from him today?

"What are you doing out here?" he asked.

She took in his Adidas shoes, running pants, and an old, ratted sweatshirt. A ribbed beanie hugged his head, his hair curling around its brim. "I think the same thing as you."

"You mean I'm not the only insane person to go running before five in the morning?" Cash held out a gloved hand and helped Gwynn to her feet.

"Oh, you are." She brushed the snow and dirt from her backside. "According to my body clock, it's almost seven."

Cash motioned to the retriever. "Sorry if Sawyer freaked you out. I rarely leash him because he sticks by my side, but this morning, he took off."

"He must've caught the reindeer's scent, came to investigate, and then I distracted him." She scrubbed the fur along the dog's back.

"You saw a reindeer?"

"Mm-hmm. A huge one. With an uncanny, calculating look." Gwynn motioned in the direction the reindeer fled. "Most impressive rack you ever saw, though."

"Montana doesn't have reindeer. You must have seen an elk."

She cocked an eyebrow. "I know the difference between an elk and a reindeer, even if I do live in the city. And that was definitely a reindeer."

Which begged the question: what was it doing around here?

A breeze picked up, and branches creaked above their heads.

Worrying her lip, Gwynn retreated a few paces and rubbed her arms in the frosty air. "Um, I should get going. It's too cold to stand still for long, and I don't want to derail you from your run. Bye, Sawyer." She turned and began a slow jog in the direction of Aunt Maude's house.

Seconds later, Sawyer dashed past her, followed by Cash, who altered his stride to match hers. "Is that your way of getting rid of me? Or may I join you?"

Gwynn shrugged. "It's still predominantly a free country, but you needn't feel obligated."

"It would ease my mind. Prospect's wild days might be far behind us, but we do have shady characters, and I'd feel better if—"

"Cash." Holding up a hand, she stopped in the middle of the walkway. "You gave the impression yesterday that I make you uncomfortable, so if you're tolerating my company because you suffer from a gentlemanly guilt trip, well … quit it."

A wan smile flitted across Cash's mouth. "It's no guilt trip.

But you're right—I shouldn't have bolted so fast after dropping you off. It was rude of me, and I'm sorry. You just—" He swiped off his beanie and ran a glove over his hair. Sawyer wandered back to nose his thigh. "You remind me of a girl I grew up with, and it threw me for a spin."

She feigned ignorance but dropped her gaze, stabbing the toe of her sneaker in a small patch of snow. "So, uh, will there be other people who wig out over my face? Should I wear a mask while visiting?" Now there was an idea. It would certainly solve any awkward chance encounters.

"A few will do a double take." Cash replaced his beanie then rubbed the back of his neck. "The thing is, Hadley Jacobs died almost ten years ago, and it's still a sore subject for people because we never learned the exact details concerning her death."

"Ah." Gwynn stared at the yellow halo from the lone streetlamp marking the edge of Bentley Park. *Lord, why did you bring me out here?* "Were you two close? That must have been hard for you."

"We'd actually had a falling out a few weeks before she …" Cash swallowed and gave Sawyer a scratch behind his ears. "It's complicated. But we didn't get the chance to make amends."

This needs closure. Uncle Russ's words from last night described the current vibe rolling off Cash's shoulders. Gwynn's chest tightened. Good gravy, he didn't continue to long for Hadley, did he? She'd made decisions specifically so that *wouldn't* happen.

"I'm sorry," she whispered.

What a hollow ring those two words often had.

"Thank you. Sometimes it's a battle to leave it in the past, but God's been faithful to help me heal." He glanced at her. "I'm not pining for her, in case you're wondering. She was a teenage crush."

"Oh. I …" Gwynn rubbed her arms again. Surely, she couldn't be *that* transparent.

Cash ducked his head with a self-conscious laugh. "Or maybe

you weren't wondering." He peeked at her through lowered lids. "Maybe I wanted to make sure you knew."

Her cheeks heated, the warmth seeping into her heart despite the fact he was not part of her plan.

Cash cleared his throat and gestured down the path. "Shall we continue?"

"I'm actually heading back to the Davisons' place."

"Then allow me to escort you there. Please?"

The sincerity and concern in his tone trounced her willpower, and she released a smile. "Okay, fine. But only because I suspect your inner gentleman wouldn't let you live it down if I refused."

"You'd wound his pride, that's for sure."

"Yeah, well, with this kind of chivalry, you're going to ruin *me* from dating any other guy." She slapped a mitten over her mouth. Shoot, she'd done it again. "That came out wrong. I'm not implying you and I are dating. Obviously. I mean, for all intents and purposes, we barely know each other. Not that if we knew each other better, we'd be dating, of course—" Gwynn pulled the brim of her hat over her eyes. "Say something so I stop talking."

"Why? This is fun."

"Shut up."

Cash chuckled. "You want to sprint back to the Davisons' with me? Sprinting at high altitudes should leave a Bostonian wheezing and speechless in no time."

She shared his grin. "Let's do it."

Chapter Eight

"IF YOU *find yourself with nothing to do this afternoon, feel free to swing by the shop. Take a look around. You never know what may inspire your own creativity."*

Cash's words to Gwynn before they parted ways at the Davisons' front porch swam in her mind on perpetual repeat as she showered, dressed, gave Holly a quick update over the phone, and descended the stairs to see what the kitchen offered in the way of breakfast.

She didn't know about inspiration so much as the excuse to enjoy Cash's company a little more. A pleasure she couldn't afford.

"This dude sounds too good to be true," Holly had said a few minutes earlier. "You better not leave there without snagging his phone number."

"Remember my rule about guys and their numbers."

"I know, I know." Holly's voice reflected the eye-roll Gwynn couldn't see. "He's got to ask for your number first. I'd say it's a stupid rule, except you have decent luck with it. Your dates start out with potential, at least."

"Yet I'm still single." And she always would be. Liars didn't deserve a happily-ever-after.

Then it's time to face the truth.

Gwynn shoved aside the thought as she reached the base of the wide staircase. *Not now, Lord.*

She checked the front living room, where the Christmas tree bathed Santa and the surrounding area in a soft yellow glow, then padded across the central hallway to the dining room. Finding no one, she moved down the hall with its lineup of Christmas trees toward the back of the house and entered the kitchen.

Aunt Maude looked up as she poured herself a mug of coffee from the coffeemaker, Brisket hunkered by her feet. "Good morning, Gwynn."

"Morning."

The dog's ears perked, and he scurried to greet her, jumping on his hind legs to paw at her knees. Gwynn crouched and rubbed under his chin. "And good morning to you, Brisket." She grinned up at Uncle Russ, who leaned against the countertop, legs crossed at the ankles, sipping from a cup with "Glacier National Park" printed on its side. "That smells heavenly."

"Would you like a cup?" Aunt Maude opened a cupboard door above the coffeemaker and at Gwynn's nod, she removed a ceramic mug.

"Leave extra room for cream, please." Gwynn gave Brisket a final pat and stood, once again admiring the kitchen with its recently renovated white-washed oak cupboards, ivory granite countertop, and reclaimed barn wood floor. It had sported a 1970s vibe the last time she'd been here, in a terrified daze, years ago— the dazed part according to Uncle Russ. She, herself, didn't re-member, nor did she want to. "Are there any plans for breakfast? Otherwise, I'm content with having cereal."

Handing Gwynn her coffee, Aunt Maude looked sidelong at Uncle Russ. "We were hoping to treat you to breakfast at Verdie's Vittles."

Gwynn smiled her thanks as Uncle Russ offered her the pitcher of cream but shook her head at her aunt. "I'd gain too much attention there, which is the last thing we need." The cream swirled and expanded in the black liquid. "When I went for a run this morning—"

"I told you I heard her up and about at a ridiculous hour," Aunt Maude said to Uncle Russ. To Gwynn, she added, "So, you got in a bit of exercise already. Good for you."

"If you call a labored jog exercise." Gwynn took a sip of coffee then set her mug on the counter. "Anyway, Cash Cooper and his dog were also out for their morning run."

"Oh?"

"Yeah. I kinda called him out on his hasty departure yesterday, and he admitted I remind him of Hadley Jacobs." She rubbed a thumb along the puckered scar on her left hand. "Despite my different hair and eye color, and the passage of time."

Uncle Russ shielded his reaction behind a long pull of coffee while Aunt Maude blinked at Gwynn, unruffled. "Okay."

"It's not okay. The only reason Cash hasn't figured things out is because God must be blinding him. But I can't expect God to blind everyone."

"Those who cared about Hadley may note similarities," Uncle Russ said. "Most everyone else will be oblivious."

"Besides"—Aunt Maude withdrew a bag of dry dog food from a lower cupboard—"you can't hole up in here for the next two days until you go back to Boston."

"Why not?" Gwynn turned a pleading look on Uncle Russ. "My plan in visiting did not involve me traipsing around town like a resurrected ghost, giving people nightmares." *Or giving myself nightmares.*

"Can ghosts be resurrected?" Aunt Maude scooped dog food into Brisket's metal bowl next to the fridge as Brisket wagged his tail in anticipation. "And can you have *night*mares during the daytime?"

Uncle Russ cradled his mug against his chest. "You might have made this trip with one purpose in mind, Gwynn, but God brought you here to do more than humor an old man. Don't squander this opportunity."

Gwynn huffed. "What opportunity?"

"To heal."

"You said that last night. I'd have to rip off the scab first."

"Good." Aunt Maude gestured to Brisket, and he dashed to his bowl. "Better to clean out the infection that way."

Gwynn trembled, her eyes wide. "You knew. You two knew I might be forced into an uncomfortable situation if I came here."

Uncle Russ studied his coffee, but Aunt Maude's chin rose. "So did you. Deep down. But I'll admit my reasons were partly selfish in getting you to visit." She glanced at her husband, moisture collecting in her eyes. "I don't want this to continue hanging over Russell's head, sweetheart. When he does die someday, I want it to be with a clear conscience."

Uncle Russ patted his wife's cheek. "No one is dying, love."

"Not right now, no. But we're not guaranteed tomorrow." Aunt Maude plunked the bag of dog food onto the countertop, her face taut. "I don't mean to be difficult, Gwynn. On the one hand, with each passing year it becomes easier to ignore the decisions we made. On the other hand, the weight of it gets heavier."

Guilt twisted Gwynn's insides like a hand fisting a rope, and she sagged against the counter. "I hadn't thought about this being so taxing for you both. Perhaps *I've* been the selfish one."

"Then maybe it's time to sort this out." Aunt Maude fingered a strand of Gwynn's bottle-blonde hair. "You're creatively blocked. Your career's stuck. You keep any romantic interest at arm's length. If you want to move into a promising future, Gwynn, you need to deal with the past."

Gwynn pressed her palm against her breastbone, her pulse quickening. "What if that reveals the *true* nightmare? Are we prepared to deal with the consequences?"

"Now you listen to me." Aunt Maude cupped Gwynn's face, her own wrinkled one growing steely. "Don't think for one minute that we'd have jumped through certain hoops if we believed you capable of your worst-case imaginings."

Uncle Russ jabbed his mug in the air, coffee sloshing over its rim. "You are not a monster, young lady."

Gwynn blinked back tears and whispered, "There's a reason I don't remember what happened."

Chapter Nine

IN THE end, Gwynn convinced them to stay in for a pancake breakfast despite Aunt Maude's mumbling about missing out on Verdie's cornbread.

And after breakfast, they convinced Gwynn to take some pie to Cash at Plane & Knotty Carpentry.

"Don't let fear hold you hostage in this house," Uncle Russ said. "But, if it would make you feel better, you could wear my balaclava to cover the lower half of your face. It's cold enough outside, no one would think twice about it."

She passed on the balaclava but wore her scarf over her nose as she trekked toward Broadway. In her hands she carried a plastic-wrapped plate heaped with a fourth of Aunt Maude's huckleberry pie. How had her plans altered so much in twenty-four hours? She'd spent almost the entire last decade avoiding thoughts of Cash, yet in less than a day in his relative proximity, she'd already begun mooning over him. She hadn't even put up a fuss when tasked with delivering the pie!

Okay, so Cash was a hot handyman with a chivalrous streak. That kind of guy existed in Boston, right? She simply had to try harder in seeking him out. They wouldn't have shared history like she had with Cash, but that wasn't a requirement for a successful relationship.

Up ahead, a church came into view, stalwart in its classic, rectangular structure and white clapboard siding. Gwynn bit her lip.

Shared history? Not necessary. Faith in God? An absolute must.

The steeple rose tall and straight, stretching toward the blue sky. A graveyard sprawled along the church's west and south sides, its headstones dotting the snow-covered grass. Bare tree branches flexed over the graves, creaking in the breeze, and an older man stood beneath one, studying a headstone.

An older man wearing a red and black plaid jacket.

It couldn't be.

"Excuse me!" Gwynn called out, changing her course to step off the sidewalk and into the graveyard. "Sir?"

He looked up, and her steps faltered. It *was* him! The Santa-double who'd bought her painting a few days ago. What was he doing here? He acknowledged her with a nod then turned and strode in the opposite direction, deeper into the graveyard.

Where was he going? "Sir, wait! Please." Clutching the pie plate, she hurried after him, wending her way between headstones. Her foot snagged on a squat grave marker, and she almost biffed it. With quick side hops, she kept her balance *and* kept hold of the plate. Whew! Grinning, Gwynn resumed her trek toward—

He was gone.

She spun around and peered through the trees lining the graveyard. "Hello?" How had the man disappeared so fast? Why did he keep evading her? First at the Bozeman airport and now here.

Gwynn scrubbed her eyes with a mitten. "Or maybe I'm losing my mind," she mumbled, pausing at the spot where he'd been standing. "Lord, keep me sane on this trip." She glanced down at the simple arced headstone before her and gulped at the name inscribed on its gray face.

Hadley Jacobs
One life that touched many hearts.
Always loved. Never forgotten.

Her pulse thudded. It was like an out-of-body experience, seeing her birth name etched on a grave. And yet, the stone didn't lie, for in one sense, she had died all those years ago.

"Was she a friend of yours?" asked a voice from behind her.

The Santa dude! Gwynn turned, and her grin fell. A stranger stared at her, his gloved hands gripping a metal detector. One thick scar disfigured the man's upper lip, and a toothpick jutted between his teeth.

A tremor raced down her spine in realization. Not a stranger, after all. "N-no, she wasn't a friend."

The man's eyes narrowed, and he stumbled forward. "You look like you coulda been her sister."

She looked like …? Dangit, her scarf had slipped. Backing away, she hiked the fabric over her nose. She couldn't afford to have this man recognize her. "Not her sister, either."

He jutted his chin at her. "Who are you, then?"

"Nobody. No one special."

"Everyone's special to someone. You got a someone?"

Gwynn shook her head, her hand securing the scarf.

The man pointed at Hadley's headstone with the metal detector. "I heard money was lost right a'fore she died. A'fore they all died. Or hidden, maybe. And that she had somethin' to do with it." He jiggled the toothpick with his teeth, his gaze shrewd. "What do you reckon 'bout that? You back for the money?"

Her heart knocked against her ribcage, and Gwynn glanced

toward the street. Empty. Drat. "I-I don't know what you mean. If you'll excuse me, I've got to get going." She moved to put a tombstone between them.

"You scared o' me, lady? I ain't gonna hurt you."

"No, no, it's not that," she lied. "But people are expecting me, so"—she hoisted the pie, as though that explained everything— "have a nice day." Gwynn made a beeline for the sidewalk. At the far corner of the church, she glanced back. The man continued to watch her, his toothpick bobbing between mashed lips.

With a shudder that had nothing to do with the weather, Gwynn hurried the last few blocks toward the Plane & Knotty barn. She didn't slow until she barreled inside and shut the door behind her.

Collapsing against it, Gwynn expelled a breath and lowered her scarf as she stared at the ceiling lights. *Thank you, Father, for keeping me safe.* Charlie Parker had never hurt her, but as one of her father's former lackeys, he likely didn't have clean hands.

The muted drone of a power tool in a back room pushed past her thoughts, along with paws pattering on the floorboards. From around an oak desk, Sawyer came charging and barreled into Gwynn's legs. Laughing, Gwynn stooped to receive a lick on the chin.

"Hey, boy. You remember me, huh?" She removed her mittens one at a time, careful to keep the pie out of Sawyer's reach, and ruffled the fur at his neck. Then she straightened and glanced about, tucking her mittens into a coat pocket.

A myriad of furniture pieces jostled for attention in this front room. Whether stained or unfinished, each one appeared more visually stunning than the last: dressers and desks, tables and bookshelves, benches and stools and chairs. In the spirit of Christmas, mini-evergreen trees perched atop some pieces, while garland and festive picks adorned others.

Gwynn drifted among the beauty, her hand gliding over

smooth surfaces, polished edges, and dovetailed corners. Tears collected in her eyes at the craftsmanship, and she let out another laugh. "It's foolish to get emotional over furniture," she told Sawyer as she opened a hutch door.

"It means you know quality when you see it."

Her tummy flipped at the baritone, and she whirled around. The power tool no longer hummed. Instead, Cash stood in the back doorway, wiping his hands on a stained towel, his blue gaze assessing. He wore a leather tool belt slung low around his waist, and cowboy boots peeked from beneath frayed jeans.

Her throat went dry, and she curled her fingers over the lip of the plate, its rim digging into her ribcage. "Hi."

"Hi." Cash propped a shoulder against the doorjamb and smiled. "I must admit I had my doubts you'd actually come by, but as you can see"—he hooked his thumb into his tool belt with a wink—"I was prepared on the off chance you did."

Gwynn's cheeks flamed. She thrust the plate forward, balanced on her palm. "Aunt Maude asked me to deliver this. I'm not interrupting anything, am I?"

"Just working on a custom order. Thank you." Cash took the offering, their fingers brushing under the plate, and Gwynn whipped her hands behind her back. He gestured around the room. "What do you think?"

"Of your shop? It's wonderful." She skirted a walnut end table beside her and inhaled the wood notes lingering in the air. "These pieces are gorgeous. When you said you were a carpenter, you totally downplayed your talent."

"Thanks." Cash set the plate on a nearby child's desk then scratched the dark scruff on his jaw. "Speaking of talent, yesterday you mentioned painting mountains on a living room wall, or flowers on a frameless canvas, and it hit me. That's what my furniture is missing. What would you think about painting scenes on a couple of my pieces?"

Gwynn's eyebrows rose. "Paint on furniture? Yikes. *Maybe* to turn one man's trash into another man's treasure, but these pieces"—she spread her hands to indicate the furniture—"are already treasures. You don't want me ruining your work with silly pictures."

"You wouldn't be ruining it. You'd be *enhancing* it." Cash went to the nearest secretary desk and framed the center of its drop front face with his forefingers and thumbs. "Imagine a country scene here. Or"—he moved to the coffee table opposite the desk—"a winter scene on this surface. You could transform my 'plane' wood into gems."

Gwynn stared at him. "You've put way too much thought into this."

"I'll pay you. That vendor I met with yesterday would go nuts over the idea."

"It's a bad idea." Walking between two rows of bureaus, she glanced back over her shoulder. "Even if it were a good one, we couldn't implement it. I live two thousand miles away."

Cash opened his mouth, blinked, closed his mouth again, and jammed a hand through his hair. "Right."

"But why wouldn't the vendor like these pieces as-is?" She moved down another row. "You're a gifted craftsman. You'll have a booth at the Christmas Jamboree, won't you?"

"Yeah. We don't sell a ton of furniture at the Jam, but we drum up enough business from custom orders to keep us busy through the spring."

"That's gre—oh, good grief, I can't seem to get away from you." Another three-foot, red-robed Santa stood beside a squat metal mailbox, "Letters to Santa" printed on its side in curlicue font.

"What do you have against Stanley?" Cash asked, coming up behind her.

Gwynn choked. "That is *not* his name."

"Gramps named him a few years ago. Stanley has a permanent spot in our shop, and kids come in all year round to mail their letters."

I used to be one of them. Back when Stanley was plain ol' Santa. She straightened the mannequin's spectacles. "Lately, I keep running into some rendition of the jolly fat man, be he animate or inanimate."

"You make it sound like a bad thing. Were you a naughty child, Gwynn Sadler?" Cash teased.

She turned to a tall dresser nearby. "Define 'naughty.'" She peeked inside a middle drawer as the front entrance whooshed open, and cold air blew through the shop. Cash moved away, presumably to greet the newcomer.

"Hey, Handsome," a female voice sing-songed.

Gwynn stiffened, but the dresser blocked the woman from view.

Footfalls suggesting sensible, winter boots strode across the floor. "I'm taking an early lunch break and brought you a treat from the café." A paper bag *shooshed* with its contents followed by a bubbly laugh. "Although, you could consider it a bribe since I might need you to run interference between your sister and my customers. Ainsley's scowl is enough to scare the roast out of my coffee beans. What's this about you shackling her to this 'stupid little town' for the rest of her life? What happened to—oh." The woman had stepped into Gwynn's line of sight, and Gwynn braced for impact as the woman swept her from head to toe in an apprising look.

If Gwynn had known she'd run into both Alex Jacob's former lackey *and* Hadley's childhood nemesis on the same morning, she would have never ventured past the Davisons' front porch.

Chapter Ten

"TESSA, THIS is Gwynn Sadler." Cash took Tessa's treat in one hand and extended his other toward Gwynn. "Gwynn, this is Tessa Reynolds. She manages The Nutty Bean coffee shop a few blocks away."

Looking cute in a white puffer jacket, black leggings, and trendy UGG boots, Tessa offered her a warm smile. "Nice to meet you."

Gwynn had never been on the receiving end of Tessa's genuine smiles, so even though she smiled in return, Gwynn clenched her jaw to keep it from falling open in shock. Yet, why should Tessa's kindness surprise her? Tessa had disliked *Hadley Jacobs*; to the girls posing no threat to her love interest, however, she could afford niceties.

"As to Ainsley," Cash said, addressing Tessa, "this morning, she showed me the financial package for the college she wants to attend next fall, and I informed her a carpenter's income only stretches so far. That's why she's grumpy."

Ainsley was getting ready to graduate high school? She'd been a nine-year-old squirt with deep blue eyes and lots of potential before a certain night had devastated so many lives.

"I'm sorry." Tessa laid her hand on Cash's forearm. "No luck, then, when searching for your father's money this past weekend?"

"Nope. I'm starting to think this is a fool's endeavor."

"Your father's money? Is that connected to—" Gwynn pressed her knuckles to her mouth. "Sorry. Another person had mentioned money and … Never mind. Thinking out loud again." She needed to invest in heavy-duty duct tape.

Tessa tilted her head. "You look familiar. Have we met before?"

"This is Gwynn's first visit to Prospect," Cash said. "She's staying with the Davisons."

"Oh?"

Gwynn linked her hands behind her back. "I'm their great-niece."

Delicate lines formed in Tessa's brow. "So, you're adopted."

Cash coughed. "Tessa."

"I don't mean to be blunt." Tessa held up a placating hand. "But you know my mother, Cash. And she knows everything about everyone in this town. Russell Davison had a sister who got married but couldn't have kids. Which means she couldn't have had a granddaughter, and therefore Russell …" Tessa shrugged at Gwynn.

Bravo, Tessa. Gwynn lifted her chin. "Yes, I'm adopted. Russ's sister, Edith, and her husband, Jeb, adopted me when most couples their age were enjoying retirement. And I'm forever grateful to them."

"That's sweet." Another warm smile. "I am sorry for prying, but when something in my little corner of the world doesn't make sense, I tend to ferret out why." Tessa's speculative gaze moved over Gwynn again, and then she turned to Cash, curling her hand around his bicep. "What are you up to right now? I thought you could join me at Verdie's Vittles for my break."

Was Aunt Maude wrong and these two were, in fact, an item?

Cash kneaded the back of his neck. "I can't leave the shop while I have a customer, Tessa."

"Don't stay on my account." Gwynn pulled on her mittens, her gaze falling away from the picture-perfect couple. "I should get going, anyway. Enjoy your lunch." She maneuvered around furniture to the entrance and glanced through the lone front window. Christmas garland swung in the light breeze where it spanned Broadway, and—

She sucked in a breath and ducked behind a tall dresser.

Cash's forehead puckered. "What's wrong?"

Gwynn chose her words carefully. "There's a guy across the street. I saw him on my way here. He … doesn't give off the best vibes."

Tessa peered out the window. "That's Charlie Parker. He's harmless."

Maybe. Maybe not. "Then why is he loitering?"

"He's not loitering. Like Cash, he searches for buried treasure."

"I don't search on concrete sidewalks," Cash said, his tone affronted.

Tessa's laugh bubbled up a second time. "I said Charlie was harmless, not smart." She tugged at Cash's arm. "Let's go. My lunch break's only an hour."

Cash studied Gwynn long enough she finally broke eye contact. He slipped from Tessa's hold. "Sorry, Tess. Another time." He nodded to Gwynn. "I'll walk you home."

"You will?" Gwynn blew out a breath. "That would be great."

He picked up the pie plate and the treat Tessa brought. "Let me hide these from Gramps in case he returns before I do, and I'll grab my coat."

"Lunch tomorrow, then?" Tessa called after him.

"We'll see," he called back.

Tessa sighed, glanced at Gwynn with a polite smile, and left the shop.

Gwynn sagged against the dresser, her emotions snarled in knots. She'd often wondered growing up if she and Tessa would have become friends, had Cash not been in the picture. Tessa seemed nice enough now that Gwynn wouldn't fault Cash if he eventually fell for her.

Tessa *Cooper.* Gwynn winced at the bad taste in her mouth.

"Ready?"

She started at Cash's voice. He emerged from the back room, tugging on his gloves, his Stetson in place.

"Yes, thanks." She looped her scarf around her chin. "Sorry to inconvenience you, though."

"I'm happy to walk you back." Cash ushered her outside and locked the door behind them.

From underneath an awning, Charlie watched them. Cash touched his hat brim, nodding at the shady man, and took her arm to lead her diagonally across Broadway. The warmth of his gloved hand seeped through Gwynn's coat sleeve as they headed for a side street one block south of the church.

"I've never known Charlie to harm anyone," Cash said in low tones, "but I wonder if you should mention this to Russ. Just in case." He dropped his hold once they reached the side street.

"Uncle Russ retired from the force two years ago. What good would it do, other than make him worry?"

"I'm guessing sheriffs are like the Marines." Cash turned up the collar to his Carhartt jacket. "Once an officer, always an officer."

Gwynn grinned. "After Poppa Jeb passed away, Uncle Russ became a type of father figure to me." *I owe my life to him.*

"In what way?"

"Hmm?"

"You said you owe your life to him."

"Oh." Gwynn skidded on packed ice and Cash gripped her elbow to steady her.

"Another slip of the tongue you didn't mean to let *slip*?" He chuckled. "You must drive your customers and housemates crazy with that odd habit."

"It's not usually this bad," she grumbled.

"Well, I'd love to hear the story … whenever you're ready to tell it."

They walked in companionable silence for a while, Cash's hand occasionally brushing against her mittened one. It may as well have been skin-on-skin contact for the way her heartbeat skittered.

He took a deep breath. "I want to apologize for Tessa's needling earlier. Adoption can be a touchy subject, and I'm sorry if she provoked you into admitting something you weren't ready to share."

Did he apologize because he felt responsible … because Tessa was his girlfriend? "It's fine. People learn of my adoption eventually."

He took her hand in a casual hold. Her pulse raced in a very *non*-casual manner. So, maybe Tessa wasn't his girlfriend?

"Did the Sadlers adopt you when you were a baby?"

"No, I was older. Though I managed to dodge the foster care system."

"Oh?" Cash cocked his head as they turned onto the Davisons' street. "Do you know your biological parents, then?"

"I … did."

"Past tense?"

She nodded once. In her peripheral vision, Cash gave her a sidelong look as if expecting her to continue, but she compressed her lips between her teeth so she wouldn't accidentally blurt something else. Their conversation already veered too close to the uncomfortable.

Cash squeezed her fingers. "I'm sorry for your loss."

They approached the Davisons' house a moment later and made their way up the front walk to the porch. "There's a lot I won't find out about you before you leave on Thursday, is there?" Cash asked.

"You know more about me than most guys I date." Christmas garland hugged the porch handrail, and she batted the snow crystals clinging to its fake needles.

"Now there's an idea."

"What?"

"A date." Cash turned her to face him. "Will you have dinner with me tomorrow?"

His pale gaze pierced her under the brim of his Stetson, and her insides flipped. *Steady, girl.* "Aren't you with Tessa?"

"No." Cash held up their linked hands. "I wouldn't openly flirt with you if that were the case. I'm a gentleman."

"So you claim. But that's all I have to go on right now—your word and a few examples from yesterday." Combined with all the memories she *hadn't* locked away. Gwynn wriggled her hand free and ascended the steps.

"She's not my girlfriend," Cash said. "You heard her. She was stopping by with a treat."

Gwynn pivoted on the top step, looping an arm around the porch post arrayed in more garland. "She was hoping for a lunch date."

Cash removed his hat and studied its interior. "It's true that she's interested in me. But I don't know how I feel in return."

"Yet, the possibility exists for you two." Gwynn adjusted a berry spray fitted among the garland as her spirits fell. She shouldn't care. She was leaving in two days.

"Maybe." Cash propped his foot on the second step and

looked up. "I'm at the point where I want to find a girl to share my life with. I'm ready to get married, start a family, pursue common dreams and future hopes."

Gwynn studied Cash's face, made all the more handsome by his confession. He deserved such an outcome. She had once longed for it, as well. But while Cash ticked all the right boxes, he was off-limits to her. "Do you realize how unusual it is for men your age to desire marriage and a family?"

"About as unusual as women my age."

"Which makes Tessa an attractive option."

"What about you?"

"Me?" Gwynn's heart bounced at the implication. "You mean … would *I* make an, uh—"

"An attractive option?" Grinning, Cash replaced his hat and ascended a step. "The *attractive* part is obvious. But I'm wondering when you hope to settle down."

She brushed her mitten back and forth over the garland needles. "As a child, I wanted to get married young. Like, right out of high school." Escape her pre-Sadler life. "I'm now twenty-four and suspect that marriage isn't in my future."

"Why not? If it's because gentlemanly admirers are, as you said, scarce in Boston, then move here." Cash climbed a second step. "I guarantee you'd have at least one admirer."

Not if he knew the truth. She retreated toward the front door as he joined her on the porch. "You're better off with Tessa."

Cash rubbed a gloved hand along his jaw. "Funny. Hadley said the same thing about another girl when we were in high school."

"Did you take her advice?"

"No."

"Why not? If you did, you might be married by now."

"Maybe I wasn't interested in that other girl." Cash's gaze held hers. "Maybe I'm not interested in Tessa. I already told you I feel a connection with *you.*"

"You'd end up disappointed."

The corner of his mouth lifted, and he moved closer. "Is that what you say to all the guys who take an interest in you?"

"Only those who matter," she whispered, backing against the doorjamb.

A pleased spark lit his eyes. He inched forward until their boots almost touched. "You know you said that out loud, right?"

Gwynn nodded, catching his woodsy scent.

Cash gave her a slow, toe-curling smile. His focus dipped to her lips. "You haven't answered my question about dinner."

Not part of the plan. That's what she should say. More time with him meant more opportunities for him to recognize her.

"Tomorrow's my last evening with the Davisons, so I'm having dinner with them," she said. *Good job, Sadler.* "Would you like to pop in for dessert?" Whoa—where'd that come from?

But what could it hurt to enjoy this man's attentions over a sweet treat? She'd fly back to Boston soon enough and have the rest of her life to corral her treacherous emotions.

"Dessert it is."

Cash leaned in and Gwynn swayed forward, her stomach tripping over itself. Their gazes tangled, his eyes sharpened, he reached around her and—

He opened the front door. It swung inward on silent hinges. "You should get inside and warm up," he murmured, sweeping a strand of hair from her cheek with a gloved finger. "I'll see you tomorrow."

Warm up? Could she get any hotter? "See you." Clutching the doorjamb, she turned to escape before her jelly legs gave out on her.

Chapter Eleven

"I DIDN'T think they made guys like him anymore," Holly said early the next morning when Gwynn called and updated her on the previous day's events. "Does he have a brother? A cousin? I'll be on the next flight out if it means I can meet me some real men."

Propped against the headboard in the guest room, Gwynn studied the dark mahogany dresser against the wall. "You don't have to exhaust yourself or your bank account trying to meet the right guy, Hols. He'll find you. Be patient."

"Patience is overrated. But, whatever. Will you see Cash again before you leave?"

"He's coming for dessert tonight." And she hadn't been able to dislodge his idea of painting designs on furniture. Even now, a vision of oversize, brilliant blue orchids gracing the side of the dresser bloomed in her mind's eye.

"Ooo. Going to meet the 'fam,' huh? This is serious."

Gwynn laughed. "Would you stop? He already knows the Davisons. And one dessert is as serious as we're ever going to get."

"You admitted you wanted to kiss him, Gwynn. You've never felt that way about any guy you've dated, let alone one you've known for *two days*."

Two days plus the first fifteen years of her life. "So, I'm attracted to him. Doesn't mean I follow my hormones willy-nilly." She shifted on the bed so she couldn't see the dresser.

"Why not?"

"Because we live two thousand miles apart. Because—as you pointed out—we barely know each other." Anymore. And should he ever learn the truth, his interest in her would shrivel faster than the dried fruit on Aunt Maude's DIY Christmas ornaments.

"Those aren't deal breakers, Gwynn. They're obstacles to overcome—and easy ones at that."

"I don't deserve a guy like Cash in my life. And God knows Cash deserves way better than me."

Holly sighed. "You don't give yourself enough credit when it comes to relationships. Why is that? You're an amazing person. You have this faith in God that even I, as an atheist, envy."

"Hols—"

"Ah, ah, I'm not done. You're compassionate, selfless, caring, a hard worker, responsible, conscientious. What's not to love about you?"

"Plenty."

"Give me one example."

Did she dare? The Davisons were the only people remaining who knew her secret. Would Holly treat her differently if she knew? It had happened so long ago, and yet it felt fresher than ever.

A knock rapped on her door, and Aunt Maude poked her head inside the bedroom. "I'm making tonight's dinner in the slow cooker. Want to come down and help?"

"Sure. Holly, I'll call you back later."

"Aw, *man*." Holly let out a sound as though she'd collapsed onto a soft surface. "Fine. But we're not done discussing this. And I want deets on how dessert goes tonight!"

Gwynn applied herself to whatever chore Aunt Maude needed done to keep her mind occupied and avoid thinking about Cash or entertaining the "what if's" that waltzed in her head. As she cleaned the half-bathroom, she questioned the wisdom in inviting him over for dessert … but she also envisioned painting a mountain valley on the double vanity doors. As she vacuumed the dining and living room floors, she kicked herself for not saying a firm goodbye yesterday afternoon … then she imagined a ranch scene sprawled across the surface of the Davisons' antique tea cart.

Cash had ruined her preference for simple, stained furniture and awakened her creative vision to a new realm of possibilities.

And in a few hours, he was coming here under misconceptions. She should be ashamed.

But she couldn't bring herself to seek forgiveness.

Tomorrow. She'd pick up the pieces tomorrow.

Dinnertime neared, and the slow cooker's rich smells of elk roast and potatoes permeated the downstairs. Gwynn's stomach growled as she stood at the island counter, scooping sugared apple slices into an unbaked pie shell. Apparently, the few butterscotch candies she'd snitched from Uncle Russ's snack cupboard hadn't appeased her belly. Brisket sat at her feet, tail sweeping the floor, his brown eyes trained on her and the dessert.

She grinned at him. "I'm not the only hungry one, am I?"

Soft Christmas music played from a radio in the corner, and she hummed to the familiar tunes as Aunt Maude flitted back and forth through the swinging door connecting the dining room with the kitchen.

"Could you grab me the lemon from the fridge, please?" Gwynn asked before her aunt could scurry away again.

"Hmm?" A water pitcher in one hand, Aunt Maude opened the fridge and set a ketchup bottle in front of Gwynn.

Gwynn snorted. "What has you so distracted this past hour?"

"Nothing. Why?" Aunt Maude marched through the swinging door.

Gwynn shook her head, wiped her fingers on a nearby towel, and rummaged in the fridge for the lemon. The doorbell rang, and Uncle Russ's footsteps crossed the front hall to answer the door. Gwynn cut the lemon into quarters, straining to hear the muffled voices. Who would visit them at the dinner hour? Should she make herself scarce?

Aunt Maude hurried into the kitchen. "So, Gwynn, dear …"

Gwynn returned to the pie with a lemon wedge. "Yes?"

"Um … well, I, uh, called the Plane & Knotty earlier and …" Aunt Maude fingered a piece of discarded pie dough, and as the voices in the hall grew closer, she blurted, "And I invited Cash to dinner."

"You did *what*?"

Uncle Russ entered the kitchen from the central hallway. Behind him came Cash, a small flower bouquet in his hand.

Their gazes caught across the room. Her fingers twitched. Lemon juice squirted, and her left eye began to burn.

"Ow!" Blinking furiously, she dropped the lemon and rushed around the island counter to the kitchen sink. "Ow ow ow."

"Oh, sweetie, what happened?" Aunt Maude asked.

"Lemon. Eye." Tears streaming, Gwynn washed and rinsed her hands, then removed her left contact lens. So much for making a good impression this evening. After setting the contact beside the sink, she bent near the faucet to scoop water into her stinging eye. Her hair fell over her shoulder. Cash's bouquet settled on the sink's edge, and a strong hand gathered her hair, twisting it away from the water.

Gwynn angled her head to smile at Cash through watery eyes as she cupped her hand under the faucet again. "Thanks."

"You smell nice," he said.

She chuckled. "It's probably my peppermint shampoo." She glanced at the bouquet with its Christmas arrangement of red amaryllis, winterberries, and evergreen sprigs, and her smile grew. "Are those for me?"

"They are."

Her heart fluttered. "Thank you. I promise I'll admire them thoroughly once my eye stops smarting." She motioned to her face. "And once I fix my makeup. I-I didn't know you were coming for dinner. Aunt Maude sprung it on me right as you walked in."

His eyebrows rose in mock offense. "Are you saying I'm not a welcome surprise?"

"Hardly." Gwynn brought a fresh handful of water to her eye and blinked several times. "A girl likes to be prepared, that's all." She straightened and grabbed a paper towel from the nearby roll to dab at her face.

Cash looked up from the counter, his brow now furrowed, and peered at her. She blinked again, testing her eye. "What is it?"

He tapped a finger by her contact lens, a bright green against the ivory countertop. "This isn't your natural color then?"

Gwynn froze, her face flushing cold then hot, and met his gaze in a knee-jerk reaction before spinning away. *Stupid girl.* How could she be such an idiot? Gingerly picking up the contact between shaking fingers, she whispered, "If you'll excuse me, I need to clean this. Be right back."

Keeping her eyes lowered, she hurried from the kitchen, the door whooshing shut behind her.

Once upstairs in the bathroom, Gwynn struggled with trembling hands to put her lens in some solution. "Calm down, calm down," she muttered. She gripped the vanity. "It might not be that bad. He might not have noticed."

With perfect vision, she stared at her reflection in the mirror. One green eye and one hazel eye stared back at her. For so long, she'd worn the cosmetic contacts around people who didn't know—or care—about her past that with the pain of lemon juice, she hadn't thought to remain guarded in front of the one person who mattered.

Had he noticed her hazel eye color? If so, would he think anything of it? Would he jump to conclusions or give her the benefit of the doubt?

Oh, please, Lord, let it be the latter.

"Foolish girl." Gwynn drilled a hand through her hair and paced alongside the tub. She shouldn't have invited him over. She should've listened to sound judgment, not given in to her weakness for Cash Cooper!

She rubbed at a dark splotch on her shirt and found several more. Water from the sink downstairs? Leaving her contact lens to soak, she went across the hall to her bedroom and changed into a wine-red ribbed turtleneck that flattered her figure. Then she replaced her lens and touched up her makeup.

Maybe if she presented a pretty enough picture, she could distract him from her blunder.

She slipped her mascara wand back into the tube and examined her reflection. Different hair color, different style. Change of eye color, the real shade he couldn't know for sure. The passage of time was on her side, too, her face having slimmed down in the last decade. She nodded approval.

"Hadley Jacobs is dead." She flicked off the light and left the bathroom. "Long live Gwynn Sadler."

Chapter Twelve

GWYNN PAUSED outside the kitchen door, Uncle Russ's voice drifting through the crack as he romanticized his latest hunting trip.

Lord, please continue to blanket Cash's vision, she prayed, imagining him with scales over his eyes like Paul on the road to Damascus. *Let him not see who I* was, *but who I am.*

She pushed open the door and stepped into the kitchen, her gaze drawn to where Cash relaxed against the counter in a button-up, midnight blue shirt tucked into black jeans over black cowboy boots. His arms were crossed, biceps bulging beneath the fabric, and his blue eyes popped. This man would cause the Mona Lisa to salivate. He looked. That. Good.

His expression brightened, and she offered him a tentative smile. "Sorry about all that hullabaloo when you walked in. So embarrassing."

"Life happens, Gwynn. You look beautiful." Cash held out his bouquet nestled in one of Aunt Maude's vases. "So beautiful, in fact, that these flowers are jealous."

Her cheeks heated as she took the vase. She inhaled the delicate notes of the amaryllis mixed with a hint of pine and cinnamon. Had the flower shop added essential oil for the holiday season? "Thank you. I love them."

Aunt Maude made shooing motions with her hands. "Why don't you kids put them on the table in the dining room? We'll be in shortly with the food."

"Do you want help carrying anything?" Cash asked.

"You're a guest. You go sit."

"Yes, ma'am."

Gwynn held the swinging door with her foot as Cash followed her into the dining room. His proximity sent her pulse zinging. Too nervous. She must calm down. Centering the vase on the table next to the water pitcher, she nodded to the place settings. "Uncle Russ will sit there at the head. Aunt Maude usually sits here." She indicated the chair closest to the kitchen then rounded the table to the two chairs across from her aunt. "Which means you and I are here."

"You didn't wonder why there was an extra place setting?" Cash asked, helping to push in her chair as she sat.

"Uncle Russ must have set the table while I was busy with the pie. He and Aunt Maude are sneaky when they want to be." She fiddled with her knife as Cash took a seat on her right, scents of cedar and clove drifting past. "Though I don't know why they felt it necessary to keep it a secret. You were already coming for dessert."

"Whatever their reasons, they did it with good intentions." Cash angled toward her in his chair and rested an elbow beside his place setting. "They clearly love you. Sang your praises after you left the kitchen earlier."

Gwynn played with her spoon. "They've been a constant in my life for a long time. Before Mama Edith and Poppa Jeb died, we'd meet up with the Davisons for a few weeks each summer, always somewhere new. Cape Cod. New Orleans. Nashville. St. Augustine."

Cash hooked his other arm over the back of his chair. "Did you ever visit out west? Estes Park? The Tetons? Las Vegas? The Grand Canyon?"

Gwynn shook her head, tucking her hair behind her ear. They'd purposely stayed east of the Mississippi River. For her sake. She swiped her hands down her jeans and stared at the door to the kitchen. Where were Uncle Russ and Aunt Maude? "What about you? Have you ever visited the east coast?"

"I made it as far as Kentucky once, seven years ago." He studied her. She sensed his attention in her peripheral vision like the stroke of a paintbrush tracing her features, and it sent frissons across her skin. "Come tomorrow, there will be a blond-haired, not-green-eyed, compelling reason to make it all the way to New England."

She smoothed a crease in her jeans with a finger. "Are you disappointed?"

"That your eyes aren't naturally bright green? Gwynn ..." His tone invited her to face him. When she did, he shifted closer. "That's not why I'm attracted to you."

She held his gaze. "Why *are* you attracted to me?" Because she intrigued him as Gwynn ... or because she reminded him of Hadley?

The door to the kitchen swung inward, and Cash straightened as Uncle Russ entered, Brisket bouncing at his feet. He held open the door for Aunt Maude, who carried a wide platter heaped with steaming elk roast and vegetables from the slow cooker.

She set the platter next to the flowers. "We just heard on the radio that a storm is expected to arrive tomorrow."

Gwynn's stomach clenched, and she bent to scratch Brisket behind the ears. "Do you think that will affect my flight?"

"Shouldn't hit until the evening." Uncle Russ added a basket of rolls and a salad bowl to the table. "You'll make it out all right."

"The real question is"—Aunt Maude sank into her chair across from Gwynn—"will it affect Friday's Christmas Jamboree preparations?"

Uncle Russ shook his head. "The storm will have blown through by then, and we've worked in worse conditions than freshly fallen snow." He held out his hands to his wife and Gwynn. "Shall we say grace?"

Biting her lip, Gwynn glanced at Cash and extended her hand. He took it with a wink before bowing his head, but as Uncle Russ prayed, Cash rearranged his hold and slid his fingers between hers. She shivered from the electric charge and didn't register Uncle Russ's words until he said, "Amen."

Sorry, Lord.

"Cash, are you and Gramps ready for the Christmas Jam?" Aunt Maude asked as they passed the food around the table.

Cash nodded, taking the meat platter Gwynn offered him. "Gramps has whittled extra Christmas trees and fat Santa figurines and bug-eyed reindeer for the children. And along with a few major pieces of furniture, I've got several small end tables and child-sized stools that should be easy sellers."

Gwynn reached for her water glass, smiling at a sudden memory. "Will Gramps dress up as Santa Claus, like usual?"

"Uh, yeah." Cash's brow knit together as he cut into his meat. "But how'd you know that's what he usually does? You haven't even met him."

Gwynn choked on her swallow of water then coughed into her napkin. "Sorry," she wheezed, exchanging a look with the Davisons. "Went down wrong."

Uncle Russ gave her an awkward pat on the shoulder. "We've probably told her about Gramps over the years. We share our news on the phone each week, don't we, honey?"

She nodded, avoiding Cash's gaze which was narrowed in thought.

After a moment he asked, "Do you sell your artwork at Christmas markets back in Boston?"

God was surely still in her corner for Cash to let the conversation move on. Gwynn smiled. "As a matter of fact, the gallery where I work, Gilded Editions, is taking part in an art show this Saturday. There's a lot of prep work involved, hence why my job is kinda on the line. I left Irene—my boss—in the lurch this week to come visit." She squeezed Uncle Russ's hand. "Not that I regret my choice. It'll pan out."

"You're selling your artwork, Gwynn?" Aunt Maude's eyes crinkled. "That's wonderful! You never said anything—"

"Only two of my prints will be for sale." Gwynn broke her roll in half. "I'm blocked, remember? I've barely painted anything in the last six months." Except for the landscape that Santa-double had bought last week.

"If you'd take me up on my offer …" Cash kicked her lightly under the table as he speared a chunk of potato.

"Oh?" Aunt Maude leaned over her plate, her loose-fitting shirt grazing her food. "What offer?"

"It's nothing." Gwynn returned his kick with one of her own. "It's not feasible, nor would I have time for Cash's flights of fancy."

Cash smirked. "My feet are firmly planted."

"But your head's in the clouds."

"I have grand ideas."

"Dreams."

"Where do you think ideas originate?"

She scoffed and buttered her roll. "Anyway, Saturday's art gala ushers in the holiday season and all its busyness. There are other craft fairs to attend, shows at the Wang Center, work-related parties … Maybe after the New Year, I'll reassess my own artwork."

"Shows and parties, hmm? Need a date for those, Gwynn?" Aunt Maude pointed a loaded fork at Cash. "He might be willing to make you another offer."

Chapter Thirteen

THEY TALKED and laughed and teased their way through dinner, save for when Aunt Maude had to rescue the apple pie from the oven. As they cleared the dishes, moving back and forth between rooms, Uncle Russ asked Cash about his sister, Ainsley.

"She's a senior this year, isn't she?" Uncle Russ set two more plates beside the sink, where Gwynn rinsed the dishes and loaded them in the dishwasher. "Any plans for college?"

"She'd like to go." Utensils clinked as Cash slipped them into the silverware basket. "But whether that's to further her education or simply get away from home, who knows." He expelled a breath and tugged at his shirt front. "I make a decent living at what I do, and I'm grateful. But I can't afford to send Ainsley to college without her accruing debt, nor is it fair for me to ask the Forresters to pitch in." He looked at Gwynn. "Erik and Dani Forrester were best friends with my parents and became Ainsley's and my legal guardians when our parents died."

Gwynn pretended the news was unknown to her. Pretended

she didn't also know Dani and her mother, Vivian, were sisters, making the Forresters her biological aunt and uncle.

Aunt Maude scooped grounds into the coffeemaker for a fresh pot, its caramel aroma filling the room. "What does she want to study?"

"Business." Cash took the last plate from Gwynn and set it in the dishwasher. "She wants to open a coffee shop geared toward high school and college age youths. Whatever that entails."

"Lots of techie stuff," Gwynn said.

Cash chuckled. "You're not wrong."

Uncle Russ removed four matching mugs from the cupboard and motioned for them to follow him back to the dining room. "Do Ainsley's college aspirations mean you're still searching for that treasure?" he asked Cash.

"Again with the treasure?" Gwynn grabbed the carton of cream from the fridge and hurried after the two men. "Does it actually exist, or is it a local fairy tale?" Had Charlie Parker been referring to this treasure when he'd asked her about the money?

"It exists," Cash said as Uncle Russ put the mugs by their places. "My dad had been working for Alex Jacobs, Hadley's father, at the time. Dad was an honest ranch hand—not like the other miscreants Alex employed—and had been digging new post holes along Alex's back property line when he found the … well, the buried treasure."

Aunt Maude whisked into the room, plonked the pie on the table, and whisked away again. Gwynn went over to switch on the Christmas Story lamp before taking her seat. "What happened to the treasure, that you're having to search for it now?" She tucked one foot under her leg with a frown. "How does one lose something like that?"

Cash puffed out his cheeks, rubbing the handle to his mug with his thumb. "Technically, my dad didn't lose it. Alex stole it from him. And"—he tilted the empty mug toward him—"Hadley stole it from Alex. Who knows where it ended up."

Gwynn's world tilted with the mug, and her breathing stalled. She'd done *what?*

Uncle Russ sat back in his chair. "I never heard that bit of information."

"Oh. Yeah …" Color seeped up Cash's neck. "I may not have told Officer Keyes *everything* that happened that night."

"That night?" Uncle Russ crossed his arms. "Are you saying you knew about this when your father was killed?"

Gwynn's heart batted against her ribcage, and she forced herself to take normal breaths. Aunt Maude reentered with the coffee carafe and four dessert plates. Placing the items on the table, she squinted first at her husband then at Cash. "What'd I miss?"

Cash let out a self-conscious laugh and ran his hands down his thighs. "I think I'm about to get into trouble."

"I'm retired, son. And the case is cold." A muscle pulsed in Uncle Russ's temple. "Still, you should start talking."

Gwynn put her hand on Cash's arm and gave Uncle Russ a significant look. "He doesn't have to if he doesn't want to. Like you said, the case is cold." And maybe she didn't want to learn what Cash would reveal.

Cash cleared his throat. "I appreciate that, Gwynn, but since it's part of my past, it informs my future, and you may as well hear it from me than the rumor mill." He poured himself coffee, his gaze moving from Gwynn to Uncle Russ. "Everyone knows I went to the AJ Ranch that evening hoping to talk to Hadley, and that when I arrived, I found Hadley's parents already dead and my father dying." He tapped a finger against his cup. "What no one knows is that I caught my father's last words … and witnessed Hadley fleeing the house."

Aunt Maude froze in the middle of handing Uncle Russ a piece of pie. "You saw Hadley … *fleeing?*"

"Yeah. We'd broken up a few weeks earlier, after I found her making out with another guy." Cash took a sip of coffee. "Once the initial shock wore off, though, I couldn't let things end without talking it over first. We had too much history between us."

With halting movements, Aunt Maude slid a piece of pie in front of Gwynn, one in front of Cash, and sat down with her own piece. Gwynn poked at an apple slice, her stomach roiling.

Cash pulled his plate closer. "As I was about to knock, the front door opened, and Hadley barreled outside. Into me. She'd been crying." He sunk his fork into his crust. "She had blood smeared on her cheek, her sweater, her hands. I didn't know what to think. She tried to run past me, but I caught her arm and asked what happened."

He gazed across the room toward the Christmas lamp. "'It's my fault,' she'd said. 'Please forgive me.' I demanded more details, but she kept repeating the same words, over and over. Then Dad called my name from inside the house. That's when Hadley broke away and started running. I almost took off after her, but Dad called again, and I went inside." Cash's throat convulsed. "There was so much blood. Alex lay a few feet away, lifeless. Vivian's body ... also lifeless.

"I cradled Dad's head in my lap and asked who had done this to him. 'Hadley,' was his answer. 'Hadley's got the money. She took it. Hid it.' Dad made me promise him I'd find it, but who cared about money? I wanted to know who shot him. He became incoherent after that, mumbling half-phrases that didn't make any sense. And then ... he was gone. A good man, a godly man ... gone."

Silence followed his words. Gwynn's eyes burned as she stared at her pie. *Lord ...? How ...?*

Cash's mother, torn up with grief, had died a few months later. Gwynn had cried when the Davisons told her the news. It was the last time she'd allowed them to talk about the goings-on in Prospect or update her on anyone from her former life.

She should be thankful Cash's account of *that night* hadn't conjured up any memories. Lesser, inconsequential memories were clanging to get free, but the others … the others she'd locked in a separate cage, buried deep, and thrown away the key. She grieved Cash's loss, yet even more, she feared the ramifications if she remembered the missing details.

Beside her, Cash sucked in a breath and straightened. He glanced around the table. "I'm sorry," he rasped, his voice thick. "I didn't mean for the conversation to take such an ominous turn."

Gwynn shook her head. "Don't apologize. Ever. What happened to you is unthinkable. How you've managed to thrive after what you saw is incredible. *You're* incredible."

"I didn't get where I am today without a lot of divine help, prayers, and support from people who cared about me." Cash brushed a crumb from the tablecloth. "Don't put me on a pedestal, Gwynn. I'm far from perfect."

He was closer to perfection than she was. *It's my fault. Please forgive me.* Had she actually said those words? They could only mean one thing … couldn't they? Gwynn pushed away from the table. "If you'll excuse me, I need to use the restroom."

She escaped into the hallway, moving out of sight around the corner, and staggered against the wall. Blinking at the tin-plated ceiling, she bit down on her knuckle. She *was* a monster! And she had caused so much pain.

"Sorry I didn't divulge this information at the time." Cash's voice drifted into the hall. Gwynn held her breath. "Looking back now, I should have. I don't know why I didn't."

"Maybe you were subconsciously trying to protect Hadley," Uncle Russ said. "Her words certainly raise suspicion."

"But the autopsies—"

"Yes, the autopsies exonerated her." Uncle Russ's voice was muffled, as if he scrubbed a hand over his face. "Although Alex's Glock bore her fingerprints."

"Hadley didn't kill anyone," Aunt Maude declared, a fork clinking against a plate. "Russell, you said there was evidence someone else had been at the house, so the fact is, even after what Cash has told us, we still don't know exactly what led to the shoot out or who stabbed Alex."

"And any hopes to know the truth," Cash added, "died the day Hadley did."

Chapter Fourteen

"THANKS FOR coming," Gwynn said softly a while later, walking Cash to the front door as the Davisons retreated into the kitchen. She handed him his coat from the coat tree with a tight smile. "I'm sorry we dredged up painful memories for you."

Conversations had changed to lighter topics after she returned to the dining room, but although they'd joked through a round of Canasta, Gwynn couldn't shake Cash's account of *that night.*

"It's all right, Gwynn." He shrugged into his coat. "No, it's not my favorite topic for discussion, but talking about it is part of the healing process."

"I don't imagine a child ever fully heals from losing a parent too soon."

"Maybe not this side of heaven. But it's true what the Bible says—for everything there is a season. A time to weep and a time to laugh. A time to mourn and a time to dance. I've done my share of mourning. I'm ready for a new season." He gently took her hand and drew her closer. "One that I hope involves getting your phone number. I'd like to stay in touch with you."

"Why?" She blinked up at him. "Given what you shared tonight, how can you stand to be around me when my face reminds you of … *her*?" The monster.

Cash toyed with her fingers, and heat spiraled in her belly. "You asked earlier why I'm attracted to you. We haven't known each other long, but from what I've seen, you have a compassionate heart, a quick wit, an adorable habit of speaking your thoughts aloud, my dog likes you—"

"Dogs like everyone."

"—and you love the Lord." His thumb moved over the back of her hand. "I think that's my favorite character trait."

She bit her lip. "You're making Boston look less appealing by the minute."

"Good. Though I hear the Freedom Trail is pretty cool." He grinned. "I could use a tour guide when I come out to visit."

"*When* you come?" That would be heavenly. And horrible.

His focus dipped to her mouth, and he nodded, sliding a finger under the cuff of her sleeve. Shivers of pleasure tiptoed up her arm. "What do you say? Is it a date?" A funny expression stole over his features then. He glanced at their hands as he drew lazy circles along the inside of her palm.

Gwynn froze. Her *left* palm. The one with the raised scar running across the base of her thumb. A scar she'd seen every day for the last thirteen years so that it no longer registered—yet was a complete giveaway.

She began to pull her hand back, but Cash's fingers tightened, and he nudged aside her sleeve cuff to reveal more of the scar.

"What is this?" he whispered.

"I-it's nothing. A childhood injury."

His gaze raked over her in accusation, the memory—oh, yes, she knew exactly what he was thinking—playing out across his face. Her body went cold then hot like earlier in the kitchen, and she gave another tug on her hand.

The muscles popped in his jaw. "I'm going to ask you this one time, and as God is our witness, I want the truth. Are you Hadley Jacobs?"

She wet her lips but looked him in the eye. "My name is Gwynn Sadler. I'm not that girl you once knew." *That* girl had died at her own insistence one late spring day. Gwynn pulled against his grip. "I told you, this is from a childhood injury."

"What kind of injury?"

"Please let me go."

"Did it happen when you went fishing, perhaps?"

"Let. Go."

Face hardening to granite, Cash released her, and she yanked her cuff over the scar.

He stood at the door, his breathing heavy, scrutinizing her like he might scrutinize a plank of wood to use for a project. Was she worth keeping … or did he throw her in the scrap bin?

"When were you adopted?" His words shot like nails from a nail gun.

She retreated a step. "Excuse me?"

"You said you weren't a baby when the Sadlers adopted you, *Gwynn*, so how old were you? This is not a difficult question."

"It's also none of your business."

His nostrils flared, and his eyes pinched with … hurt? Anger? Confusion? Denial? All of the above?

Lord—

She stopped, her heart clunking inside her chest. This was her mess. She had deliberately taken advantage of every minute Cash hadn't recognized her. She'd known it would end—had to end—but she'd intended to be long gone when it did.

Just because those hopes now curdled like DIY chalk paint gone awry, she couldn't ask God to pluck her from the wreckage.

"Your facial features resemble a dead girl," Cash growled low. "You wear bright green contacts to mask your real eye color—

hazel, perhaps? You've a freckle on your right cheekbone. Like *her*. Your dark eyebrows don't match your blonde hair. I noticed at dinner that you eat left-handed, and now I find you have a familiar scar on that very hand. Heck, you even use peppermint shampoo. Purely for the holiday season, I reckon, like *she* did. This explains a lot, actually."

Cash lifted his hat from the coat tree, his eyes freezing into shards of ice. "Did you ever feel like a disciple on the road to Emmaus, walking and talking with a loved one whom you were shielded from recognizing?" He set his hat atop his dark waves and reached for the doorknob. "Me, neither. Until now." He jerked open the door. "Excuse me. God and I are about to have some words."

Gwynn sank onto the bottom tread of the staircase as Cash's truck roared to life and peeled away. She rubbed her thumb along her puckered scar, glaring at it through watery vision.

She'd been eleven, Cash thirteen, when they'd gone fishing one summer afternoon in the stream behind her house. She'd slipped on a slimy rock and landed with a shriek in the stream bed, cutting her hand on a jagged edge.

An intense stinging burned her palm, and she shrieked again, staring at the blood pooling in a gash along the base of her thumb.

"Jiminy Cricket, what's the matter with you?" Cash splashed up behind her and plucked the fishing pole from her other hand.

"I'm gonna die!" Blood trickled down her wet arm and dripped from her elbow to swirl in the water around her. Bile crept at the back of her throat. "I fell and ripped my hand open and now I'm gonna die." She glared at Cash, who peered at the wound. "Why'd we come fishing, anyway?"

"'Cause you like to fish, silly." He grimaced and poked her skin.

She jerked away. "Don't do that!"

"It looks bad."

"Duh!" She grasped her wrist, and her eyes stung along with her hand. "I'm dying."

"Don't be so dramatic. You're not dying. We'll take you home and—"

"I don't want to die!" So. Much. Blood! Her breath came in pants. "I'm only eleven! I haven't done anything *with my life. I haven't been* anywhere. *What about going to Europe and becoming a world-famous painter and getting married and having lots of kids? I haven't even been kissed yet!"*

Cash rolled his eyes, leaned in, and planted his lips on hers. "There. You've been kissed. Now will you shut up? My mom can fix your hand. For now, we'll wrap it in something. You really want to leave this great fishin'?"

"Cash Cooper, you big jerk!" She shoved his skinny bare chest with her good hand, and he stumbled backward, nearly toppling into the waters himself.

"Hey! What was that for?" he yelled as she stomped toward the embankment, cradling her hand.

She kicked water in his direction. "Next time you go kissing a girl, ask her permission first."

Later, Cash would claim he'd taken her advice, though the next girl he'd kissed had been a lab partner from his eighth-grade science class. But after Hadley entered high school as a freshman, Cash—then a junior—had pulled her into the shadows behind Gramps' kiosk during the Christmas Jam and asked her permission. She'd given it, and they'd exchanged a kiss sweeter than the chocolate fudge his parents had bought them earlier.

They dated until she'd staged that kiss with Prospect's star soccer player, Travis Phillips, at the Valentine's Day dance a year later.

"And now I've hurt him all over again," Gwynn whispered.

… He can't stand cheating. But how else could I prove that he's wrong to waste his emotions on someone like me? In time, he'll see it's better we go our separate ways.

The lines from a long-ago letter floated in her mind's eye, and Gwynn rubbed her temples. To whom had she written those words?

Gramps. She had snuck, unnoticed, into his barn workshop one evening about a week after the dance and slid the letter into his Santa mailbox. The last nod she'd given to "Santa Claus."

She'd had but one Christmas wish that year, and he hadn't answered it. Why not? Gramps loved Cash like the grandson he'd never had. Wouldn't he have wanted to see Cash happy with a girl worthy of his affections?

"Well?"

Gwynn peeked around the balustrade. Brisket scampered down the central hallway toward her on his short legs as Aunt Maude stood in the kitchen doorway. She wiped her hands on a towel, eyebrows raised in expectation. "How did it go?"

"About as well as my worst fears." Gwynn fisted her left hand. Ignoring Brisket's pleas for attention, she pushed to her feet and climbed the stairs to start packing. "I knew I should've stuck to my original plan."

Chapter Fifteen

"I'M SO sorry," Holly said the next morning when Gwynn called her. "You … you want me to, uh, pray for you?"

Gwynn grunted, righting her newsboy cap over her Dutch braids. "I suppose my misery can't be all that bad if you're willing to start a conversation with God."

Holly laughed. "It'll be good to have you back. Am I picking you up at the airport, or are you taking an Uber?"

She peered through the bedroom curtain at the snow whipping about outside. "I'd love to see a friendly face when I arrive in Boston." If her flight didn't get canceled because of this storm.

"Then I'll meet you at the airport. See you tonight."

They ended the call, and Gwynn dropped the phone into her backpack. As she hoisted the bag onto her shoulder, the vase with Cash's bouquet on the bureau caught her eye. She fingered a red amaryllis petal. It didn't matter how much chemistry they had— some things weren't meant to be.

Seizing the handle to her carry-on, she left the room and

clambered down the stairs. Another gust of wind rattled the windows, and she shuddered. The storm had arrived much earlier than expected, but Uncle Russ promised he'd get her to Bozeman. After last night's disastrous ending, she had more incentive than a mere job calling her back to the east coast.

She needed to escape Prospect—and Cash—all over again.

But while Uncle Russ had left no reason for anyone to look for her the last time she'd fled, would Cash hound her and demand answers this time?

"He'll be disappointed," she grumbled, rolling the carry-on to the front door. "I have none to give."

The household phone jangled in the hallway behind her, and she jumped, placing a hand to her heart. An odd thing to have in a home these days, even if it blended with Aunt Maude's nostalgic decor from a bygone era.

Uncle Russ emerged from the living room on the third ring and picked up the receiver on the fifth. "Hello? Oh, good morning, Cash." His eyebrows rose in Gwynn's direction. Her stomach flipped like a flapjack at breakfast.

"Oh, that's not necessary," Uncle Russ said after a moment. He frowned at the ceiling. "I can't let you do that. If anything happened—"

Gwynn approached him. What could Cash possibly want after the way things ended between them?

"Can't argue with you there," Uncle Russ said.

"What's he saying?" Gwynn whispered, but her uncle raised a hand.

"Are you sure?" Uncle Russ nodded. "Understood. See you soon."

He hung up, and Gwynn gestured to the phone. "What was that about?"

Uncle Russ pulled at his mouth. "Cash will be here in a few minutes. He's going to drive you to Bozeman."

"What? No!"

"The storm caught us by surprise, Gwynn, and now the roads are atrocious. Cash is our best option for getting you to the airport. He has better reflexes and a powerful truck. You'll be safer with him than with me."

She clutched his shirt sleeve. "You know that's not true."

Uncle Russ placed his hands on her shoulders and leveled her a look. "You two need to talk."

"He's hurt. And angry."

"And who can blame him? But you're safe with him, even when he's angry. He loved you."

"He loved Hadley. He doesn't love Gwynn. If anything, he despises her now."

"Change your name all you want, it's your soul that draws him."

Cash arrived ten minutes later, a fierce gale chasing him into the house. Snowflakes clung to his eyelashes and to the fibers in his coat and knitted beanie. Gwynn gripped her arms, her heartbeat erratic as he nodded to the Davisons and greeted Brisket who jumped at his legs for attention. Lastly, he turned to Gwynn, his light blue eyes cautious yet friendly.

Her defenses slid into confusion. What happened to his anger?

"It's crazy out there," he said. "You sure you want to do this?"

"Yes."

"All right." Inclining his head, Cash grabbed her carry-on. "Say your goodbyes. I'll meet you at the truck. But be quick. Every minute we delay costs us on the roads."

Holding his collar closed at the throat, he ducked outside, and Gwynn enveloped both Aunt Maude and Uncle Russ in a group hug. "As desperate as this trip began, and as fast as it's ending, I'm grateful I got to see you two. Take care of yourselves." She crouched to scratch Brisket behind the ears but narrowed her eyes at Aunt Maude. "And no more trickery to get me out here."

"No, missy. You have my word."

Uncle Russ kissed the top of her head. "We'll come visit you in the spring, okay, kiddo?"

"I'd like that." After another round of hugs, Gwynn wriggled her hands into her mittens, shouldered her backpack purse, and exited the house.

She entered a whirlwind of white.

Wind gusts drove the snow sideways and raked her cheeks and nose as she stepped off the porch. Using her scarf as a shield, she fought to stay on the walkway, several inches deep in snow, and followed Cash's footsteps up to the road.

As she approached the truck, Cash hopped from the driver's side, jogged around, and opened the passenger door.

Her eyes widened. "Thanks. You didn't have—"

He cocked a brow.

"Right." Compressing her lips, she tossed in her backpack and climbed onto the bench seat. The door shut behind her. Heat blasted from the air vents, and the wipers swished back and forth as wet flakes splatted against the windshield. Once resettled behind the wheel, Cash pulled away from the curb.

Minutes later, they turned onto an empty Main Street, and Gwynn's mouth formed an 'o.' "Where is everyone?"

"Most of them were smart and stayed home today."

"Ah." She coughed. "You didn't have to take me to the airport. Uncle Russ was—"

"Russ is fifty years my senior. He has no business driving in these conditions." Cash looked at her askance, taking his time traversing the road. "I wouldn't be out here, either, except I heard a job was on the line."

Heat crawled up her neck. Irene *had* threatened her job, but was getting back to it worth risking these blizzard conditions?

Her job meant money, and she needed that money to pay her

bills. Her suite mates needed the money to help pay the rent. And she needed whatever contacts her job—and the exposure in this upcoming gala—might bring about for her career's future.

So, yes, she'd take the risk to reach the airport.

In silence, they made their way through town and into the wide, ranching valley beyond it. Without buildings or mountains to block the wind, the storm grew to whiteout conditions, eclipsing the pavement beneath a blanket of snow and masking the drop-offs beyond the shoulders in drifts level with the road. Cash clenched the steering wheel in both hands, tension emanating from his body.

Gwynn prayed for safety.

Cash rotated his head from side to side. "How about a game of This or That to distract me?"

He wanted to play a game? Wouldn't he rather rail about her true identity? "I don't think I want you distracted." She could also do without a tongue-lashing, however.

The side of his mouth quirked. "Coffee or tea?"

"Coffee, of course."

"Mountains or ocean?"

"Um, ocean."

"Victorian or condo?"

"Condo."

Cash snorted. "You're lying."

Gwynn peeled off her mittens. "I live in Boston. I like the ocean and small-home living."

"Where the only mountains on your horizon are 'made of brick and steel,'" Cash said, quoting her words back to her.

"I didn't say the city was my *dream* location."

"Then what is?"

She shook her head. "It's not an option."

"Fine." He shifted in his seat. "Let's see … hunting or fishing?"

"Fishing." She fingered her scar as she spoke.

"Carpentry or plumbing?"

Gwynn frowned. "What are you playing at?"

"Answer the question."

She pulled a piece of fuzz from a mitten. "Carpentry."

"Facial hair or clean shaven?"

It was her turn to snort. "Would that be for myself or the guys I'm attracted to?"

"Definitely the latter."

A few butterflies in her tummy stirred. Why wasn't he angry and confronting her? She took in the dark scruff along his jaw, her fingertips tingling, then looked away. "I prefer clean shaven."

"You're lying again."

And why shouldn't I? Lies saved my life.

"What do you mean?"

She pulled her gaze from the window. "Hmm?"

"You said lies saved your life. How is that possible?"

"I said—" Gwynn threw up her hands. "Why can't I keep my mouth shut around you? You're like my Achilles' heel."

"Listen, Gwynn—"

"No, it's my turn." She rotated to face him more fully. "Mountain cabin or coastal cottage?"

"But—"

"*Mountain cabin or coastal cottage?*"

The lines about his mouth tightened, but he said, "Barn workshop."

"Rich or poor?"

"Contented."

"Thin or fat?"

"Fit."

Gwynn glanced heavenward. "I thought you knew how to play this game."

Cash grinned, but his eyes held a challenge. "Ask me about hair color."

"Yeah, you don't know how to play." She sighed. "Okay, blondes or … redheads?"

"Brunettes."

Her heart kicked. Her natural hair color was brunette. She crushed the mittens in her lap. "Brown eyes or green?"

"Hazel."

Gwynn's gaze flew to his. They played a new game now, the truth hanging between them like an ugly portrait no one wanted to address but couldn't ignore. She wet her lips. "Rancher's daughter or"—Tessa's face flashed in her mind—"pastor's daughter?"

"Childhood sweetheart."

She swallowed around the ache in her throat. Did she dare …? "Love or hate?" she whispered.

Cash took her hand and smoothed his thumb along her scar. "I choose forgiveness."

Tears sprang to her eyes. "Cash—"

A dark shape materialized through the snow ahead, and Gwynn clutched the dashboard with a shriek. The beast reared, a red-clad figure astride its back.

Cash wrenched the steering wheel. The truck swerved, lost traction, and plowed into the shoulder of the road, its front end sinking into deeper snow.

"Oh crap oh crap oh crap." Gwynn unbuckled and spun in her seat. "Do you see them? Did we hit them?"

"*Them?* I saw a reindeer—"

"Yeah, with a male rider."

"What male rider?"

"He wore a red plaid coat—" Gwynn's jaw dropped. Red coat. White beard. "Oh, my heavens, it was that guy!"

"*What* guy?"

"The one I keep seeing everywhere. First, he came into the art gallery in Boston. Then he knocked into me at the airport in Bozeman. Then, I saw him at the—" She bit off the word *cemetery*.

Cash rammed a hand through his hair. "I don't know what you're jabbering on about, but we've got a problem."

"I'll say. We may have hit an old man."

"We didn't hit anyone—or anything—because I drove off the road instead." Cash gestured out the window. "*That's* our problem. I gotta see how bad it is." He reached into the backseat and collected his knitted beanie and gloves. "If you hadn't insisted on leaving, this wouldn't have happened."

"You're blaming me for wanting to catch my flight? I thought you understood—"

"Oh, I understand job responsibilities and wanting to please one's boss." Cash yanked on his hat and shoved his hands into his gloves. "What I don't understand"—he pinned her with his stare—"is how you can once again abandon loved ones who are still reeling from the first time you ran away." He reached for his door handle. "Stop running, Hadley Jacobs, and come home already."

Chapter Sixteen

AS CASH retrieved a shovel from the bed of his truck and attempted to dig out the front wheels, Gwynn's thoughts and emotions swirled like the snowflakes outside. Too fast to grasp. Too agitated to calm. Too enmeshed to separate.

He'd said the quiet part out loud. No stuffing the paint back into the tube now.

But to suggest she come *home*? What home? Her parents were dead, the ranch most likely sold off, her childhood things gone. What could Prospect offer other than mangled memories and a black hole surrounding *that night*?

He had mentioned loved ones, as well. Did he mean the Forresters—her biological aunt and uncle and her cousins? Guilt pummeled her like Holly pummeled new clay, because blocking memories of her life in Prospect had meant blocking memories of her relatives too. Would Cash tell them she was alive? How would they react? In steely anger, like he had?

Except, so far today, Cash hadn't responded in anger. Instead, what she'd received was … well, he'd admitted it himself: forgiveness.

Cash had forgiven her.

Cash had forgiven her.

The words solidified among her spinning thoughts, and Gwynn shook her head to dislodge them. He was lying. He had to be.

She stumbled from truck against the tangle of wind, snow, and abrasive cold, and tromped through the snowdrift to where Cash shoveled behind the driver's-side tire. "I don't deserve your forgiveness," she hollered above the wind.

He looked up and scowled. "Get back in the truck. It's freezing out here."

She tucked her bare hands under her folded arms and ignored her smarting cheeks. "Why would you give it to me? I didn't ask for it."

"Gwynn, get in the truck—"

"I withheld information from you. I misled you."

"You had your reasons."

"No! I mean, yes, I did, but I'm supposed to say that. You're supposed to be furious with me. Accuse me. Call me all sorts of names. Demand explanations."

"Believe me"—Cash straightened, looking her full in the face as snowflakes caught in his lashes—"I expect explanations. But not out here in the driving snow and arctic temps. Now get in the truck."

She huffed out a breath. "Let me help."

"You can help by praying."

"Praying?"

"Yeah. Pray that my tires find traction to free us from this ditch." He returned to shoveling, and Gwynn clambered back into the truck. She rubbed her throbbing hands together. After living years in New England, she'd forgotten how fast Montana's sub-zero windchill could seep into the bones.

Cash wanted her to pray? A week ago, it would have been her first resort. But aside from little popcorn prayers, she'd barely talked to God since arriving in Prospect. She certainly hadn't given *Him* an opportunity to talk to *her.* Not when she suspected He wanted to show her the very thing she didn't wish to see.

She leaned her arms on the dash and rested her head in the crook of an elbow.

"I'm sorry for ignoring You this week. I haven't even cracked open my Bible. Forgive me. Help me …" She sighed. "Help me to work with You rather than against You. Help me," she added with a grumble, "to *want* to work with You. Bless Cash's efforts in getting this truck unstuck. May we get back on the road, so that I can make it to the airport in time." Her chest constricted. "Please, *please* let me return to Boston, Lord. I don't want to be here any longer."

A niggling of guilt stirred in the corner of her mind, but her current repentance didn't go that deep, and she batted it away.

The driver's door opened, and the interior temp dipped several degrees. "Good. You're praying," Cash said.

Gwynn lifted her head as he slid behind the wheel and knocked snow from his hat. "You might regret asking. I feel on the outs with God at the moment."

"You know what they say. 'When you feel far from God—'"

"'Guess who moved.' Yeah, yeah." She studied the front windshield, where a layer of snow had built up in the time she'd been sitting there.

Cash started the truck. "Here goes …"

Gwynn squeezed her eyes as he pressed the gas pedal. The engine revved … and the tires spun.

Please, Lord. Please, Lord. Please, Lord.

Cash tried again, turning the wheel. Again, the tires spun in the snow.

Please please please.

"Wait." Cash whipped about, reached beneath the backseat, and withdrew a blanket. He held it between them, his eyes dancing. "Traction."

Thank you, Father!

After she helped him battle the wind and stretch out the blanket on the ground behind the two front wheels, Cash tried a third time. The wheels caught, moved, and with the momentum, the truck backed off the shoulder and onto the road.

"Yes! Thank you, Father," Cash said, echoing Gwynn's thought a moment earlier. Letting out a whoop, he exited the truck and rescued the blanket.

He was two points into a three-point turn when Gwynn realized his intentions. She grabbed his arm. "What are you doing? Where are you going?"

"Back to Prospect." He shifted into drive and finished the turn.

"No. Cash, the airport! I can still make my flight—"

"I doubt planes are taking off today, even if we could have gotten you to the airport. And that's a big 'if.'" The truck rumbled through the aggressive snow, the inches piling up on the road. "The snow's coming down too fast, and these roads are too slick. No way would we have been able to navigate the mountain pass."

Gwynn released his arm and slumped against her seat.

Cash sent her a sympathetic look. "I'm sorry."

She huffed. "No, you're not. You said yourself you want me to stop running and come home. But the fact is, I'm not running. I'm living my life—just not in Prospect." She propped her elbow on the window ledge and rubbed her forehead. "Of course, now I'll have to move because I won't be able to afford rent because I'm going to lose my job because the next flight on this airline isn't until Monday—oh!" An idea took hold, and she scrambled for her phone in her bag to make an online search. "If I switch airlines, I could fly out tomorrow. It'll cost a fortune, but—"

Cash's jaw went slack. "Erik and Dani, Duke and Lainey—they all still think you're dead. Doesn't that mean anything to you?"

Gwynn fidgeted in her seat. "I only made this trip because I thought Uncle Russ was dying."

"Russ isn't even your real uncle! The Forresters are your kin, not the Davisons."

She looked up from her phone. "But Russ is the one who gave me a second chance at life. He came up with a way to protect me, which allowed me to start over, away from any potential danger." Gritting her teeth, she returned to her airline search. "As far as I'm concerned, Hadley Jacobs died nine-and-a-half years ago, and Gwynn Sadler was born. Nothing changes simply because you know they're one and the same person."

A long stretch of silence filled the cab. Gwynn peeked once at Cash. The muscles bunched in his jaw. Not a good sign.

"Let me get this straight," Cash said at last, running a hand over his scruff. "You mislead me. You lie to me. You show no remorse for the money you stole or the lives that were taken, nor do you seem to care that it wrecked a lot of people who had to pick up the pieces afterward." His words came out calm and measured, despite their heavy charges. "And even though many of us yearn for answers of what happened that night—answers you have—you're going to go on your merry way and return to living a carefree existence across the country, never sparing a thought for the loved ones you left behind ... *again*. Did I paint an accurate picture?"

Her vision blurred.

"So maybe you're right," Cash continued. "Maybe a selfish, narcissistic person like yourself doesn't deserve forgiveness." The muscles in his jaw bunched again. "But I'll try to forgive you anyway."

"Quit it!" Gwynn threw her phone into her backpack. "Quit being so sanctimonious."

"How would you like me to behave, Hadley—"

"*Gwynn.*"

Cash's hands wrung the steering wheel. "Would you rather I yell and throw a fit?"

"If it's closer to the truth."

"Don't talk to me about truth. You have no idea how furious I was last night, once I saw your scar and realized who you were—*are.*" His neck muscles pulsed. "I was furious with you for deceiving me, with myself for being duped, with God that He didn't expose your lies sooner. We duked it out, God and I, for a long time after I left the Davisons'. But He reminded me I had already forgiven you a few years ago. Part of my healing process. And He wouldn't let me renege on that. Made it clear my forgiveness shouldn't change, whether you live or die holding the answers I seek."

Gwynn laid her head back and sighed. "I don't have any answers, Cash."

"Like I'm gonna believe you when I now know you're a chronic liar."

"I didn't outright *lie* to you. I was careful with my choice of words and—"

"Stop." Cash held up a hand. "We're done with this conversation." He jabbed at the radio button. "I need to concentrate on driving."

Chapter Seventeen

GWYNN PRESSED herself against the passenger door, hands clasped in her lap, for the duration of the return drive. She had called Uncle Russ about the change in plans and texted Holly the bad news she wouldn't be flying out that day. The silence that ensued in the cab had grown from an anthill to Rocky Mountain proportions by the time Cash turned onto the Davisons' street.

What a mess. How could she fix the rift between her and Cash? Did she want to fix it? Cash was better off without her, so it shouldn't matter to her how he felt about Hadley *or* Gwynn.

He pulled up alongside the Davisons' front walk. "I'll get your things," he said, his tone flat. He left the cab, and she dropped her head in her hands.

In a few days, she'd be back in her cultivated, safe world where she could begin a similar healing process to the one she'd gone through almost ten years ago.

Eventually, she'd be fine again.

Though she suspected this time around would prove much

harder to force fresh images of Cash into the background.

Not that plunging into a new life back then had been effort-less. For a while, she had lived in constant mental conflict. Yes, she'd reveled in a do-over with the Sadlers, who loved her and doted on her in a way her birth parents couldn't, but she'd left behind others, like the Forresters and Gramps, who had loved her too.

At the time, she had soothed her inner struggle with the con-viction she couldn't return to Prospect. Showing her face again would reopen an investigation, and while she knew she wouldn't have harmed Mr. Cooper, Cash's dad, what if she'd harmed her own father? What if the answer landed her in jail? Feeling justified in her own reasoning, she had buried the memories of her past along with her emotions and moved on as Gwynn Sadler.

"Because you're a coward," she muttered to herself. "And therefore, still a disappointment."

Maybe she hadn't done much healing, after all.

"It's disappointing—"

Gwynn yelped and jerked upright. She frowned at Cash standing with the passenger door open. "How long have you been there?"

"It's disappointing how you're going about this," he said, his voice tender, "but that doesn't make *you* a disappointment."

She growled. "I wish you'd stop listening in on my thoughts."

A tiny smile tugged at the corner of his lips. "When you stop voicing them, I'll stop listening." He held out his gloved hand. "C'mon."

But she slid from the truck without his help. The less contact with him at this point, the better.

"Gwynn? Cash?" Uncle Russ shouted from the front porch through the gusting snow. "Thank goodness, you're safe."

"Yes," Cash called out, "but stay there. I'll bring her things to you."

Slinging her backpack onto her shoulders, Gwynn followed Cash, stepping in his footprints to the front porch, where he set her carry-on by Uncle Russ's feet. He turned around and plowed into her.

He grabbed her upper arms before she toppled backward. "Sorry." Their gazes collided, lingered. Then he released her like she'd stung him. "Goodbye, Gwynn. I hope everything works out with your job, but don't look to me for another ride." He glanced at Uncle Russ and back to her. "I won't help you leave again."

As he tromped up the walkway, fresh conflict warred within her. Was this how she wanted things to end?

She hurried after him. "I don't remember what happened!" she hollered into the storm.

Cash halted, his posture stiffening.

She stopped a few feet behind him, huddling in her coat against the wind. "I don't remember that night or any other within that two-week period. My subconscious is obviously protecting me for some reason. You said yourself I admitted it was my fault."

Turning, Cash squinted at her through the snow. "You're not a killer, Hadley—"

"Gwynn."

His mouth mashed shut.

He made to go once more, but Gwynn blurted, "Please don't say anything to anybody, okay? Especially not to Aunt Dani and Uncle Erik."

"Are you kidding?" Cash closed the distance between them until he stood a pace away, his hands clenched. "Dani came to see me at the shop yesterday. She'd heard from Tessa that you looked like Hadley, and suddenly her hopes from years ago were resurrected with the idea that you could *be* Hadley. She wanted my opinion. I said it was impossible. We were at your funeral, for goodness' sake." He turned up his coat collar at another blast of wind. "We saw you get buried. Still, Dani asked me to watch you last night for any signs that you might be Hadley.

"But I didn't want you to be Hadley, doggone it." His voice grew tight. "For one, it made no sense. You. Were. Dead. And I wanted that season of my life to remain dead too. I'd already dealt with the emotions, the unanswered questions—"

"Great, then leave them there in the past. Nothing needs to change. I don't want—"

"You know what your problem is?" Cash took that last step, bringing them toe-to-toe, and pointed a gloved finger in her face. "You don't trust God to work things out in your favor."

She whacked his hand aside. "Easy for you to say. You're the poster child for Heaven. Mr. Perfect, himself."

His gaze warred with hers, pale eyes as frosty as the air blowing around them. He shook his head. "Have it your way." He whirled on his heel and strode to the truck.

Gwynn glared after him, snowflakes pelting her face and mingling with unbidden tears.

Uncle Russ wrapped an arm around her shoulders and steered her toward the front porch. "You're wrong about Cash, honey. He about drove himself crazy after his dad died, followed by his momma. Had to crawl his way back to good health and a restored relationship with God. It took even longer to restore relationships with his sister and friends."

Gwynn swiped the moisture from her cheek. "What are you talking about? What happened?"

"Let's get inside, and we'll chat over coffee." He rolled her carry-on across the porch. "Perhaps it was wrong of Maude and me to indulge you for so long, letting you sever yourself from Prospect. We didn't want news to trigger a wrong memory, but it's causing more harm than good now."

She slumped against Uncle Russ as they entered the house. "I've turned into a despicable person, haven't I?"

"No more than the rest of us needing grace."

The next morning, Gwynn spent a considerable time in prayer, crying and pleading for forgiveness and courage; for God to change her heart; to soften her stubbornness; to quiet her fears. She'd eluded Him since returning to Prospect, convinced she could bend His will to hers instead of the other way around, but after she'd tried and failed that morning to book a flight to Boston in time for the art show tomorrow, she had to face facts: God wanted her to stay.

For now, anyway.

She squirmed at what this might mean for her job and the loss of potential contacts, but what could she do other than repeatedly lift it to the Lord … and defer to His plan?

"Oh, be honest, Gwynn," she said, sitting on the bed, head down, knuckles at her forehead. "You're grateful for the excuse to stay." A certain blue-eyed someone had momentarily taken priority over her job.

Last night, Uncle Russ had filled her in on Cash's downward spiral after losing first his father and then his mother. A three-day bender had led to destructive habits, and Cash barely graduated high school in the spring. He'd disappeared afterward, abandoning Ainsley to be cared for by Erik and Dani Forrester. No one heard from Cash again until he showed up, wrecked and broken, at the Forresters' doorstep four years ago.

Meanwhile, nine-year-old Ainsley had coped with the loss of her parents and brother in her own rebellious ways, becoming a constant challenge for the Forresters, who had tried to love and protect her as best they'd known how. In middle school, she chose questionable friends, and her surly actions escalated into self-harm shortly after Cash returned. God had intervened in a suicide attempt, however, and with the help of counseling, prayer, and support, Ainsley had turned her life around over the next three years into one of health and victory.

It gutted Gwynn to hear the ways that horrific night had upended two beautiful souls, knowing its ripple effects touched countless others. If she had stayed to confront the truth instead of running away, how many lives would have turned out differently?

That burden is not yours to carry, came a gentle voice.

Gwynn covered her face as tears leaked from her eyes. "How can You be gentle with me, Lord? I screwed up. I've been living as a coward all this time, fooling myself I could ignore the past *and* call myself Your child. Please forgive me."

I gave you that period of rest.

The Bible verse from Matthew flitted through her mind: "Come to me, all you who are weary and burdened, I will give you rest."

"But it's not fair. Why should I have gotten rest while others suffered?"

I decide what is fair. All I ask is that you trust and obey.

Trust. Gwynn's heart cramped. Why did that sound like a four-letter word? "I-I don't trust You," she admitted on a whisper, lowering her head as a tear dripped from her chin. She yanked a tissue from the box beside her. "I'm scared. What if I end up in jail? What if I don't end up in jail but I lose my job and career possibilities?"

Never will I leave you; never will I forsake you.

Gwynn groaned. Could that suffice? The Sunday school answer said it was better to head to prison or into a jobless future *with* God than to live in fake freedom or superficial security without Him.

Not all Sunday school answers were easy to swallow.

She tossed the used tissue onto the growing pile in the trash can. "Help me, Lord. Help me to trust You. Help me to walk in obedience, to walk out my faith." *Help me not to live in fear.*

More scripture verses flashed through her mind, ones she'd

studied over the years and tucked away in her heart. Verses about God giving her a spirit of power rather than fear; God working for the good of those who loved Him; Jesus leaving His peace with her and instructing her to not let her heart be troubled or afraid.

Gwynn tugged another tissue free and took a deep breath. Strength infused her lungs and seeped into her arms and legs.

"Light my path, Lord. Help me take this one step at a time."

Step one: apologize to the Davisons for forcing them to carry her burden longer than necessary.

Step two: apologize to Cash.

Step three: … to be determined.

Chapter Eighteen

GWYNN PUNTED little clods of snow with each step she took toward Plane & Knotty Carpentry. Her heart bobbed in her chest, buoyed by the Davisons' earlier words of support and encouragement when she'd asked for their forgiveness.

Would Cash be as quick to forgive her today? He'd offered her forgiveness yesterday in the truck, but by the time he'd left her on the Davisons' walkway, he'd again become angry and hurt.

Gwynn passed Bentley Park, where preparations had begun in the open field for tomorrow's Christmas Jam. She tightened the scarf covering her nose and mouth, lowered the brim of her newsboy cap, and peeked askance at the activities.

Dozens of people shoveled snow, assembled kiosks and tents, arranged food trucks, and set up the live band platform beside the gazebo. Along with the familiar sights came an array of childhood memories, as if yesterday's admission of her identity had opened the door to an overstuffed closet and everything tumbled out.

There were those rare afternoons playing on the jungle gym or joining a game of Capture the Flag to avoid the stress at home.

Stolen moments admiring the craft booths at the farmer's market. Finding an Easter egg hidden in an evergreen tree. Conquering the midnight Halloween corn maze. Delighting in a million twinkling lights at the Christmas Jamboree that turned the park into a winter wonderland. Relishing a heady kiss and whispering impractical promises as a teenager in love.

A small smile lifted her lips. Each memory involved Cash Cooper and his family to some degree. His parents had anchored her growing up, guiding and encouraging her when her own parents couldn't—or wouldn't. Over the years, Cash had taken on the role of encourager and champion. By the time he became a senior in high school and she a sophomore, he'd started talking about getting married after graduation, to protect and provide for her.

She'd hungered for it like her artistic side hungered for extravagant paints, yet doubts badgered her. What if Cash came to regret his vow to love, honor, and cherish her, like her own father had come to regret his wife and kids? What if she ended up disappointing Cash, as she'd disappointed Alex?

"You're a worthless piece of trash that will amount to nothin'."

Her shoulders hunched against her father's harsh words. She hadn't wanted to risk bringing Cash to that end—a man disgruntled by the path he walked, by choosing a wife incapable of helping him see his dreams to fruition. Better to leave Cash despising her from a shallow hurt early on, she had reasoned, than from a deeper wound years into a relationship.

An icy breeze whipped through her jeans, and Gwynn stuffed her hands into her coat pockets. "It was messed up. *I* was messed up. I don't deserve his forgiveness, then or now."

Yet she still wanted it.

When she entered the Plane & Knotty barn a few minutes later, Cash appeared from the back room, tugging on his jacket. Tessa stood near the entrance, the grin on her lips turning cautious when she saw Gwynn. "Hello, again."

Cautious, not jealous. Cash must not have told Tessa the truth about Gwynn's identity. Growing up, they had been each other's nemesis. She'd envied Tessa's beauty and fashion sense, and Tessa had resented Hadley's close friendship—and later relationship—with Cash.

Time hadn't altered Tessa's long-held crush, but would time eventually alter Cash's feelings in Tessa's favor?

"What do you want, Gwynn?" Cash yanked on a pair of gloves. "I thought you were supposed to be on a plane. Or did you have a change of heart?"

Gwynn lowered her scarf. "Every flight is full, from yesterday's stranded passengers to today's incoming passengers."

"So, no change of heart then."

She swallowed at the cold tone in his voice. "I have obligations in Boston. Commitments. My boss has—" She glanced at Tessa, who didn't need to know Irene had almost fired Gwynn over the phone because she couldn't make it to the gala. "Anyway, I'm now staying until Monday." She lifted her chin, shoving aside thoughts of her job. "And I was hoping we could talk."

Cash studied his gloves. "I've said everything I need to. Unless you want to buy a table or a dresser, I'll have to ask you to leave. Tessa and I are on our way to lunch, and Gramps is already at Bentley Park setting up for the Christmas Jam."

Tessa gave Gwynn a pitying glance and took Cash's arm as he motioned Gwynn back outside onto the sidewalk. He locked the door behind them and walked away, Tessa at his side.

Gwynn stared at his retreating back, her insides crumpling like a wadded piece of sketch paper. Her opportunity to make amends faded with each second, but did it have to happen with Tessa watching?

For goodness' sake, swallow your pride, she admonished herself. *The longer you take, the louder you'll have to yell.*

"I'm sorry," she called out, her voice echoing off the buildings.

Cash slowed, and Tessa frowned up at him.

"You were right," Gwynn continued, taking a hesitant step forward. "I have been acting selfishly. And what I said yesterday, and how I said it, was wrong and insensitive, and I'm so sorry."

Cash had halted while she talked, and now he turned to face her.

Gwynn wrung her mittened hands. "Please forgive me."

Tessa tugged at his arm. "Cash, c'mon."

"Just a minute." He slipped from her hold and trudged back through the snow to Gwynn. "You mean that?"

She nodded.

He studied her, and her stomach skittered under the visceral impact in those clear eyes, but she held his gaze. "Thank you," he said at last, his voice thick. "I forgive you."

Her shoulders relaxed, and she gave a small smile.

The harsh lines around his eyes and mouth softened. "What am I supposed to make of you? Once dead, now alive." He raised his hand—

"Ca-ash," Tessa called.

His brow puckered and he pulled back. "How about I swing by the Davisons' later, and we can talk, okay?"

Gwynn nodded again.

He rejoined Tessa, and they continued toward one of the eateries on Broadway, a flawless picture of self-employed entrepreneur and respected pastor's daughter.

Hugging her arms to her chest, Gwynn crossed the street and headed for the Davisons' house. She glanced back once at the couple, her lips flattening. She had no claim on Cash—she'd made her decision about their relationship long ago, and she would stand by it today. That didn't mean she had to like his choice of girlfriend.

Not that Tessa had been anything but nice to Gwynn.

She scowled.

A particular church steeple caught her eye then, rising above the rooftops on the next street over. Her steps wavered, and she changed course in that direction. After the deluge of memories she'd already let ambush her this morning, what were a few more?

Moments later, she stood before her parents' headstones. She brushed the snow from the engraved words. *Loving father. Loving mother.*

The headstones lied, but she hadn't expected the engraver to carve the truth: *Alex Jacobs, Reluctant dad, Fraudulent cattle rancher, Questionable source of income.* Or: *Vivian Jacobs, Neglectful mom, Functioning alcoholic, Town strumpet.*

Would she have been able to rise above those origins, had the Lord not whisked her across the country? Once again, she thanked Him for the safe haven she'd found with Poppa Jeb and Mama Edith.

Gwynn scanned the names on the nearby headstones. And what of Cash's parents? She wouldn't have recognized the unconditional love in the Jacobs had the Coopers not offered it first. Were they buried in this graveyard too?

Mrs. Cooper had taught her the secret to making a tasty pie crust. Mr. Cooper had taught her how to shoot a firearm. He'd even nicknamed her Hadley 'Oakley' after she'd shown natural talent and had encouraged her to practice at the shooting range to hone her skills. She'd done so … until *that night.*

Her vision blurred. Though she didn't remember the details, Gwynn knew she'd failed Mr. Cooper—and Mrs. Cooper, since she'd died a few weeks later from a broken heart.

An ache ballooned inside Gwynn's chest, and she dropped to her knees in the snow.

How could Cash have forgiven her when she'd never be able to forgive herself?

Chapter Nineteen

"MAY I join you?"

Gwynn blinked and squinted up at Cash, who stood several paces away, his forehead lined with concern. She hefted a shoulder and looked back at her parents' graves. The snow had seeped into her pant legs, and her cheeks stung. "Did you finish your lunch date early, or have I been sitting here longer than I thought?"

Cash let out a half-laugh. "A little of both." He gestured to the graves. "Were you thinking about your folks?"

"No, actually." Pushing to her feet, she cleared her throat. "I was thinking about yours." Guilt raked along her spine like claws, and she hunched in her peacoat. "I'm so sorry for your loss, Cash. Your parents were great people, and what you and Ainsley had to endure after their deaths ..." She gripped her elbows. "God should have let them live and taken me instead—"

"Don't talk like that." Cash held up a gloved hand, his expression serious. "We can't understand the ways of God or why He calls some of us Home early."

"But it's not fair. What you went through—"

"We went through hell-on-earth, yes, but it's a comfort to remember my parents are in Heaven today. You, on the other hand—" He shook his head. "Hadley, you would have *gone* to Hell."

She shuddered. Because he'd used her birth name … or because he'd spoken truth? She hadn't believed in Jesus ten years ago. Had she died then, a different eternity would have awaited her than the one that awaited her now.

"I'm grateful God spared your life," Cash murmured, his gaze roaming her face.

She clutched at her coat sleeves so she wouldn't reach out to him. He'd been quick to give a supportive sidearm hug back in the day, later adding a kiss to her temple once they started dating. She craved a hug now, but too much emotional distance separated them.

He glanced at the line of headstones. After a prolonged silence, he asked, "Who's in the casket, if it wasn't you?"

She jabbed at the snow with her boot. "It's empty."

Cash frowned. "How is that possible? I was there at the funeral."

"Closed casket. You didn't see a body."

He dragged a gloved hand over his face. "My goodness, you're right."

"Uncle Russell was both sheriff and coroner at the time. Not only did he convince people he had identified my body months after I disappeared, but he also faked a death certificate so that everyone would believe I had died."

"Is that legal?"

"For the sheriff, it is, when done on behalf of a citizen's safety."

"I stood over there"—Cash pointed to a grand elm along the side fence—"watching the pallbearers lower your casket into the ground, thinking you didn't deserve a proper burial. No murderer deserved a headstone memorial or to take up space in a church graveyard."

Gwynn fisted the lapel to her coat. "You said I didn't kill anyone."

"I believe that now. I didn't believe it then. I was reeling from grief and had convinced myself that when you claimed the events of that night were your fault, it meant you murdered my dad despite the evidence saying otherwise."

"Evidence?" She scoffed. "Most of the evidence is up here"—she tapped her head—"locked away." With her sleeve, she swept snow from a nearby stone bench and sat. "And maybe it's locked because the reality is worse than I'd like to admit."

"According to the police report, your mother and my dad died from gunshot wounds delivered by your father's revolver, which bore his fingerprints—"

"Yeah, and *he* was shot in the stomach by a Glock that bore *my* fingerprints." The cold bench seeped through her jeans, numbing her legs to match her numb mind. "I hated Alex. You know that better than anyone." She had stopped calling him "Dad" the second time his fist had drawn blood. "There were plenty of times when I wished he'd die. When I begged God to take his life. How evil can a daughter get? But day after day, month after month, year after miserable year, God ignored my prayers." She met Cash's gaze as he crouched before her. "What if, on that wretched night, I finally set about doing what God would not?"

"Okay, but"—Cash took her mittened hand in his gloved one—"Alex also had a fatal knife wound in the back."

"Still could've been me. There were no fingerprints to show otherwise."

Cash's gaze dropped to their hands. "My dad was … wearing his leather gloves," he admitted.

"Mr. Cooper wouldn't have knifed anyone."

Cash sighed. "I still say you're in the clear. The Davisons think so too." He rose and took a seat beside her, his hand tightening about hers as his eyes grew thoughtful. "Gwynn?"

"Hmm?"

"Why did the Davisons get involved in this? Why fake your death and keep it a secret all these years? What did Russ have to gain by it?"

"They did it to protect me." At his furrowed brow, she put up her free hand. "I'll explain, but I'm relaying to you what Uncle Russ told me years ago, not what I remember. Got it?"

Cash nodded.

"According to him, I appeared at his back door in the middle of the night two days after the murders, dehydrated, incoherent, and hysterical at the thought of returning home or even staying with the Forresters. By then, Uncle Russ suspected there might have been another person involved in the crime since a second, untouched whiskey glass had sat on our dining table, as though Alex expected someone else to show up. Perhaps that person would've come after me, if they'd known I survived and could act as an eyewitness."

Gwynn skimmed her boots back and forth in the fresh snow. "Because of that suspicion coupled with my hysteria, Uncle Russ squirreled me away to stay with his sister and brother-in-law—Edith and Jeb—on the East Coast. I don't remember making the initial decision to live with the Sadlers, but I never once regretted it. It started out as a temporary arrangement, yet after several months we made it permanent."

She traced a crack in the bench with her mitten. "I still had no memories about that night, and any leads the authorities had, had grown cold or brought the detectives to a dead end." Her gaze returned to her headstone. "That's when Uncle Russ faked Hadley's death certificate and provided me with a new ID. And since he claimed my deceased body had been found on BLM land months after I'd gone missing—"

"No one questioned the idea of a closed casket."

Resentment laced Cash's tone, and Gwynn angled toward him, praying he'd understand. "I flourished under the Sadlers' care. They loved me in a way I hadn't experienced before, and for that, I'll be eternally grateful. They and the Davisons could never fathom what a gift they gave me in plucking me from this place."

"Maybe so, but"—the muscle popped in Cash's jaw—"you left many hearts in tatters back here."

Her shoulders sagged. "I see that now. Aside from the obvious people, though, I didn't think anyone else cared about me. I had made sure *you* didn't care."

Gwynn pulled from his hold and stood to pace between the bench and headstones. "After the Davisons told me about your mom, I shut the door on anyone or anything having to do with Prospect and my former life. The Davisons honored that." She toyed with the ends of her scarf. "But I didn't consider what a burden this situation had become for them until the other day. Didn't know it had become a burden to *me*."

"So ..." Cash squinted up at her. "Does that mean you're ready to find out what happened that night?"

Chapter Twenty

WAS SHE ready to discover the truth?

Gwynn turned her back to Cash sitting on the bench. Stacking her hands atop her head, she stared at the mountains in the distance. A few sun rays poked through the clouds, piercing the snow-drenched peaks like a Thomas Kincaid painting. If she copied the scene onto canvas, no one would believe it was real.

"In case it matters," Cash added when she didn't respond, "you don't have to face the past alone."

His words pierced her gloomy insides like the sun rays, and her eyebrows rose as she faced him. "You'd help me?"

"Of course. What kind of gentleman would I be to abandon you now?"

"A smart one."

"A disobedient one." Cash's knee bounced several times. "When I arrived at the Davisons' yesterday, Dani's plea kept playing in my head, asking me to look for any signs that you might be Hadley. As I prayed for clarity and discernment, God told me to stand by you."

She retook her seat. "Stand by me?"

"Yeah. That's all He said." Cash looked at her. "I haven't done a good job of that since learning who you truly are. I'm sorry. I promise to start making up for it."

Her eyes smarted. "Thanks," she whispered.

"Things will work out." Cash wrapped an arm about her shoulders and pulled her close. "You'll see."

Gwynn sank against his side with a groan. "But will things work out the way I want?"

"I don't believe God brought you back into our lives just to send you to prison."

She tucked her head under his chin, the warmth of his body spreading into hers. He smelled of wood and stain and fresh air. "How did you know to find me in the graveyard?"

"I was leaving Verdie's Vittles, about to head the Davisons', when I noticed a guy in a red plaid jacket and thought he might've been *your* guy in the red plaid jacket. I called to him, but he ignored me and turned down this side street. When I tried to catch up with him, he'd already disappeared."

"He tends to do that."

"Then I saw Charlie Parker standing on the sidewalk, staring into the cemetery. Staring at you." Gwynn shivered and Cash rubbed her arm. "Charlie was one of your dad's 'partners in crime,' wasn't he?"

She nodded against his shoulder.

"Did he ever … hurt you?"

"No, thank goodness."

"He disappeared after the authorities questioned him about the murders. Didn't return until about six months ago."

"I saw him on my way to the workshop Tuesday morning. I didn't recognize him at first, but he seemed to recognize me, despite my denials. He started fishing for information."

"Do you think he wants something from you?"

She pressed her mittened hands between her knees. "The money? I hid it but can't remember where. Isn't that what you also want?"

His arm stiffened around her shoulders. "Except in my case, the money was rightfully my dad's."

Yet Mr. Cooper had found it on her father's ranch land, so technically it had belonged to Alex. What would Cash think about that, if she pushed the issue? "Will you take me to the ranch?"

"Your ranch? The AJ Ranch?"

"It's not mine, but yes, if the crime happened there, and I witnessed it, then maybe that's the first place I should visit." And if she regained her memories, then they could find the money and then … what? Split it? Burn it? Give it away?

"There's one problem." Cash straightened, forcing her to sit up, and the cold air rushed in. "We don't know who owns the ranch anymore. It went to probate since the title was in Alex's name alone, and he had no remaining kin and no will. Had he left the ranch to your mom, it might have gone to the Forresters, considering Dani and Vivian were sisters, but he didn't, so it didn't." Cash leaned forward, elbows on his knees. "The ranch eventually sold to an outsider, though no one ever moved into it."

"It's been sitting empty for almost a decade? That's perfect."

"No," he said slowly. "Empty or not, we'd be trespassing if we snooped around without permission."

"But if no one's living there to catch us snooping …" Gwynn slipped her hands under her legs and swung her feet. "It's not like we'd break in or anything. If the door's locked, we'll peek through the windows."

He shifted on the bench to meet her gaze. "And if the door is unlocked?"

Gwynn looked up and away.

Cash chuckled. "I see your penchant for bending the rules hasn't changed."

"So … will you take me?"

His lips compressed, and he kneaded the back of his neck. "It might have to wait until after church on Sunday. I'm supposed to meet Gramps at the park soon, to help set up our kiosk for the Christmas Jam. That'll take us well into the evening, and tomorrow I'll be manning the booth all day."

"And I fly back on Monday, so Sunday it is." Gwynn stood, the invisible weight on her shoulders easing with this new plan.

"Is it bad form to pray we don't get caught when we're knowingly doing something wrong?"

"You don't have to go with me." She tugged him to his feet and gave a playful smile. "I just need your wheels to get me there. If you lend me your keys, then you can stay out of it altogether."

"That's all I'm good for, huh? A set of wheels?"

She poked his bicep through his coat sleeve. "Your strength might come in handy if the door's stuck."

Cash laughed, shaking his head. "It seems I'll have to go, if only to keep you out of trouble." Slinging his arm around her shoulders again, he pivoted her toward the street. "You owe me one, Hadley-Gwynn-Jacobs-Sadler. Hey, I know—you can help me set up for the jamboree."

"I can't show my face everywhere." She ducked from under his arm as they turned down the sidewalk. "I might fool many people, but until my memories come back, I don't want to bring attention to myself. After what you shared the other night, Uncle Russ now thinks our fathers' murders might be a nasty case of greed and revenge, no other killer needed, but I'm not taking any chances."

"All right. I can respect that."

Good-natured shouts and laughter and the hum of power tools carried over the frosty air from Bentley Park. Cash took her mittened hand as they walked, like he'd done the other day.

"How about this?" he asked. "Do you recall the dance that

finishes out the Christmas Jamboree every year? Promise you'll save me a song or two tomorrow night."

"That's not a good idea, either."

"Why not?"

"Because it prolongs the inevitable."

"Which is?"

"You—me—going our separate ways." She tugged her hand, but his grip tightened.

"Here I thought God was aligning our paths."

"For closure."

"Closure on some things. Open doors on others." Cash held her hand to his chest and glanced at her sideways. "Don't shut me out, Hadley."

She wrenched free and upped her pace. "That's the second time today you've called me by that name."

"Doggone—I'm sorry!" He hurried after her and hooked a hand around her arm, coaxing her to a stop. Red stained his cheeks. "I'm sorry, *Gwynn*. But even though you go by a different name, you're still … the same girl I fell in love with."

"No, I'm not. It's been almost ten years—we've changed." She stared over his shoulder at the people going about their different tasks in the park. They'd moved on without her, and she without them. "You loved me then," she murmured, "but you don't love me as I am now."

"You've changed for the better. How could I not end up loving you?"

Gwynn met his gaze, and he gave her a boyish grin. She rolled her eyes and continued walking.

"There's still a connection between us you can't deny." Cash came alongside her and matched her stride. "Why else would I be so enthralled with a girl I thought I'd just met who lived two thousand miles away?" He pulled ahead of her, spinning about to walk backward. "Why else would I have felt like I'd known you for years when 'reality' said otherwise?"

"It doesn't matter. I won't put myself in a position where I hurt you like I did before."

"Great. I admire a proactive woman. So, about the dance tomorrow night—"

"No, I don't mean I won't hurt you. I mean I won't get close to you, where I could hurt you again." She turned down an alley between two houses to avoid the park. Being with Cash would draw too much unwanted attention.

Cash followed. "I know what you meant. I'm choosing to ignore it and hope to convince you otherwise."

"You're impossible."

He pulled her to a stop a second time and looked down at her. Her tummy tripped as usual at the jolt of his blue irises. "Are you seeing someone else?" he asked.

"Of course not."

"But you love someone else."

She snorted. "No."

"You're interested in someone else."

"*No.*"

His mouth crooked at one corner. "So, about this dance tomorrow night …"

Gwynn chewed the inside of her cheek to keep from smiling, but it must have reflected in her eyes because Cash grinned wide enough for them both.

"I'll take that as a 'yes.'" He pressed a kiss to her forehead, and Gwynn inhaled a greedy breath of his woodsy scent. Backing away, he jerked a thumb over his shoulder. "I've got to go help Gramps, but I will see you tomorrow."

She resumed her walk in the opposite direction, winding the ends of her scarf around her hands. Her emotions undulated like a Mallard caught in the waves made by a Boston Duck Tour.

Selfishly, she wanted to let Cash win her heart. To flourish beside him for as long as this season of life allowed. But what would happen come the next season of life? What if it brought more problems than solutions? What if she failed him? Or he came to regret choosing her, like her dad had with her mom? What if—

She made a face and yanked the scarf. How she wished she could shut off her brain!

"Lord, help me convince Cash that he needs to move on and choose another girl," she grumbled, emerging from the alleyway half a block from the Davisons' house. "And shield my heart so I'm not compelled to give in to his charm."

Cash deserved so much more than she had to offer.

Chapter Twenty-One

WHEN GWYNN stepped into the kitchen the next morning, Aunt Maude greeted her with a mug of coffee. "Are you ready for some Jamboree fun? I have to drop off my pie with the judges first, but then we can go wherever you wish."

Gwynn pocketed her phone, Irene's scathing words from their brief call dulling the sunlight pouring through the window above the sink. She took the mug and stared into the black liquid. "I'm not in a celebratory mood, Aunt Maude. You and Uncle Russ go have fun."

Narrowing her gaze, Aunt Maude put a hand at Gwynn's back and directed her into the dining room. "Come. We must pray. You're obviously burdened, child, but we're not meant to bear the weight of the world."

"How can I not? Irene has already run into snags at the gala and is livid I'm not there—"

"She has other workers to help her." Aunt Maude pointed to a chair.

Gwynn sat. "One would think. What if, in her bitterness, she sours my potential contacts against me?" She glowered into her coffee. She'd forgotten the cream. "I'm creatively blocked, my past is still obscured, but honestly, why worry about any of this when—should my memories return—I might find myself locked up and wearing orange?"

"One day at a time, dear. Tomorrow has its own troubles, so let's focus on the gifts today will bring." Taking Gwynn's hand between both of hers, Aunt Maude bowed her head.

As the older woman prayed for wisdom and patience and the Lord's leading, the strain in Gwynn's muscles eased, and the sorrow and hopelessness sloughed away. As she thanked Him in advance for the anticipated resolution, an inexplicable calm nestled around Gwynn like a comforting hug.

Aunt Maude finished with, "Amen," and tightened her fingers about Gwynn's. "Come to the Jamboree. Hide your face or don't hide your face—people see what they want to see—but don't deny yourself a highlight of the Christmas season."

Gwynn kissed the woman's wrinkled hands and smiled. "Christmas Jam, here we come."

"Whoops!" Gwynn sidestepped a little boy running full tilt among the crowd. From behind her scarf, she grinned after him. Could one blame him for his exuberance? Aunt Maude had spoken truth—the Christmas Jamboree was a highlight of the season, and this year's festivities held more wonder than Gwynn remembered from her youth.

As she wandered with the Davisons through the kiosks, admiring wares and occasionally talking with vendors, snippets of memories popped to the surface: Savoring the buttery sweetness of funnel cakes dusted with powdered sugar; collecting an illustrated bookmark or clay figurine from a favorite vendor; visiting the Santa Shack where Gramps shrouded his identity behind a thick wig and beard.

Cash and his parents featured among the images, with Ainsley first in a stroller, then causing mischief as a toddler, then as a kindergartner holding Gwynn's—er, Hadley's—hand, and later acting as a third wheel when Hadley and Cash wanted to hang out alone.

Gwynn's cheeks warmed at the recollection of that first official kiss with Cash behind Gramps' kiosk and a second one shared during the Jam dance in a corner of the gazebo.

Oh, dear—would tonight's dance come with a kiss?

Scowling, she flipped her Dutch braids over her shoulder. She had no business thinking about kissing Cash. Not when she couldn't commit to a future. Yet her eyes and beating heart grudgingly acknowledged he was not only a good-looking *gentleman*, but an endearing, honorable one, as well. Hard facts to gloss over.

Speaking of the charmer, there he stood, two stalls away, inside the Plane & Knotty kiosk, conversing with a woman who scrutinized the child's desk he'd built.

Her pulse quickened.

"Oh, I see Ellen." Aunt Maude waved to a woman in the crowd. "I better go say hello."

"That's my cue to find Greg and grab a cup of coffee." Uncle Russ kissed Aunt Maude on the cheek and ambled away.

"Would you like to come with me?" Aunt Maude asked Gwynn. "Or would you prefer to meet somewhere in a little while? Ellen and I do tend to prattle on."

Gwynn's gaze flitted back to Cash. "I'll meet up with you later."

"Say 'hi' to him for me," Aunt Maude sing-songed and strolled in the direction of her friend.

The heat from Gwynn's cheeks spread down into her torso. Who needed the sun, weak as it was this time of year, when she had schoolgirl infatuation to keep her warm?

Tweaking her newsboy cap, she moved toward the wooden shelter. *Lord, restrain my heart. Let me not—*

Charlie Parker lunged into her path, and she jerked to a stop. His black eyes glittered, the ever-present toothpick hanging from his lower lip. "Rumor has it yer her. Hadley Jacobs."

"I, uh—" She touched the scarf covering her nose and glanced beyond him, but he blocked her view of Cash. "My name is Gwynn."

"Why're you back?" Charlie swayed from one foot to the other in a repetitive motion, his hands flexing spasmodically at his sides. "You comin' fer the ranch? You gonna dig up the hidden money?"

She retreated a step and scanned the area. Where had Aunt Maude gone? "I don't know what you're talking about." Did Charlie know what had happened that hellish night? He'd been interrogated years ago and come out clean, but what if he'd lied to the police?

A hand cupped her elbow. "There you are, my dear."

Red plaid registered in her peripheral vision, and Gwynn looked up into the rosy face of the Santa look-alike. Relief bubbled within her. "It's you!"

His eyes crinkled at the corners. "So it is. Come try my hot chocolate." He nodded to Charlie. "Charles, if you'll excuse us."

Santa knew one of her father's lackeys?

He maneuvered her between two kiosks, through the little alleyway, and out into another lane of vendors. Humming the Jingle Bells chorus, he approached a quaint red kiosk with a green pitched roof and white trim. Behind the open window, a young woman wearing a gray woolen jacket embroidered with green curlicues handed out steaming cups to the customers waiting in line.

Did the sun shine brighter here, or was it that Charlie no longer posed an immediate threat? Gwynn glanced over her shoulder, but the man hadn't followed them. What did he want, anyway?

"Thanks for rescuing me," she said.

"'Tis a shame Charles veered from the path in his youth." The Santa look-alike beckoned Gwynn to follow him into the kiosk through a side door. "Never could get him back on the straight and narrow."

Santa's helper turned from the window and gave her a wide smile. "You must be Gwynn." A knitted Santa cap sat at a jaunty angle atop her shoulder-length, copper waves, and her ears—wait, were her ears *pointy*?

Why not, Gwynn? It's Christmastime. What better excuse to dress up as elves or Santa or the Grinch?

The old man indicated the woman with a hand. "This is Tinsel, my granddaughter-in-law."

"Meister K needed help today." Tinsel filled a candy-cane striped cup with hot liquid from a dispenser. "So, I volunteered my husband to stay home with the kids." An impish grin sprang to her mouth as she snapped a lid onto the cup and passed it to a teenager on the other side of the window.

Gwynn lowered her scarf and turned to the man. "Meister K? That's your name? Why do you keep popping up at random times and then disappearing again without a trace? Cash almost ran you over the other day!" Was it only two days ago? She had grown a ton since then.

But had she become wiser?

Meister K let out a jolly *ho, ho, ho* and helped fill two cups with liquid chocolate. "My trusty reindeer wouldn't have let anything happen to me, but thank you for worrying."

Tinsel snickered. "Blaze had a few choice words for you after the fact."

Blaze? Gwynn gave a minute shake of her head and latched onto Meister K's comment. "That's all you have to say about what happened? 'Thank you'?" She jammed her hands on her hips. "You freaked me out!"

"If you hadn't been so insistent on getting back to Boston, I wouldn't have had to interfere." He set the cups on the counter by the window, and Tinsel fitted them with lids.

Gwynn opened and closed her mouth several times, but only a squeak came out. This old man had made her miss her flight? *On purpose?* Her eyes narrowed. "Who are you?"

He dipped his chin and looked at her. "You know very well who I am."

"No." She pinched the bridge of her nose. "No, because Santa Claus isn't real. He doesn't exist."

"Well, no, Santa Claus-as-legend doesn't exist—society has turned him into an agnostic dolt." He set two more cups before Tinsel. "Santa Claus-as-man, however, is very much real, and I'm trying to answer your letter. You're not making it easy for me." He looked at her over his wire-rimmed glasses. "But then, you've always been stubborn, or you wouldn't have written me in the first place."

Gwynn straightened in the doorway. "Wait, wait, wait. Supposing for the moment that your mental health isn't in question, what letter are you talking about?"

Meister K patted his coat pockets. "'Tis true that at the time, you didn't know you were writing to me. But it came nonetheless." He checked his pants pocket and then shuffled through a stack of napkins. "Now, where did it go?"

"You didn't leave it at the Workshop, did you?" Tinsel asked with a quirked eyebrow.

He puffed out his cheeks, his eyes twinkling. "I really need to retire."

Matching his mirth, Tinsel pressed a striped cup into Gwynn's hands. "Here. Enjoy my mother's drinking chocolate."

"*Drinking* chocolate?"

"Melted gourmet chocolate mixed with milk. I added a shot of butterscotch in yours."

"I love butterscotch," Gwynn murmured.

"I know." Tinsel winked.

Gwynn's gaze ping-ponged between the two Christmassy people before her, her thoughts muddled and sluggish. The dry mountain air, perhaps? "Have I stepped onto the set of an upcoming Hallmark movie?"

Meister K chuckled again. "I'll get that letter to you in another day or so. Promise me you won't leave Prospect before then."

"That's it? You brought me over here to … give me a letter you don't actually have? Answer my questions with more riddles? Evade them altogether?"

"Or maybe I invited you here to taste the finest drinking chocolate in the world." He gestured to her cup. "Try it."

Suppressing an eye roll, Gwynn lifted the container and took a sip. The creamy, buttery flavor slid over her tongue in a chocolate caress, and she closed her eyes, sagging against the doorjamb. "This is phenomenal."

"Even better when it doesn't come from a dispenser." Tinsel handed two more cups to customers and waved at a little boy. "But I'll send along your compliments. Drinking chocolate is my mother's signature treat."

"And now, you'd best return to your young man." Meister K moved to the side door. "He's waited all morning to see you."

Gwynn frowned. "If you're talking about Cash Cooper, he isn't mine."

"And whose fault is that?" Meister K huffed. "Don't know the last time I worked so hard to make a Christmas wish come true." He gestured for Gwynn to exit the kiosk. "Off you go, then, child. And remember."

She backed into the cold. "Remember what?"

"That's for you to figure out." Eyes twinkling, he closed the door with a, "Merry Christmas!"

Chapter Twenty-Two

GWYNN GRUMBLED to herself as she wended her way back to the Plane & Knotty kiosk. Of all the Santa doubles, she had to keep crossing paths with the most obtuse one. He had a letter for her, did he? Probably a generic Christmas card. And to his claim of being the legit Santa Claus, she said, "Bah, humbug!"

At least he'd extracted her from an uncomfortable confrontation with Charlie. She lowered her scarf for another sip of cocoa, and a reluctant smile lifted her lips. And he *had* introduced her to the best drinking chocolate ever.

A moment later, scarf in place, she entered the kiosk. Cash smiled from where he sat on a stool behind the makeshift checkout counter. Carved figurines lined the shelves on a five-tiered storage rack in the front corner, and several furniture pieces were strategically arranged on pallets. Business cards and a candy dish sat atop the counter. Other than Cash, however, the shelter appeared empty.

She returned his smile with a fleeting one of her own. "Gramps isn't around, is he?"

Cash gave a half-laugh. "You're safe. He left for his shift at the Santa Shack."

"Oh, whew." She walked between the furniture, loosening her scarf from her neck as she went. Much better.

"You should go check it out," Cash added. "The shack has been spiffed up since we were teens, and Gramps's costume looks pretty convincing."

Gwynn shuddered. "No, thanks. I've had my fill of Santas for the day."

His eyebrows hiked. "Aren't we a Scrooge-ette."

"Sorry." She gravitated toward a space heater blasting warm air from a back corner. "I had the weirdest encounter just now, and I'm not sure what to make of it."

"Care to share?"

"Not particularly." Nursing her cocoa, Gwynn stretched her free hand toward the heat. "Tell me about your morning, instead."

Cash joined her near the heater but faced the shelter's open side. "I sold a child's desk, a side table, and a small dresser. Several people have taken my business card, and Gramps's figurines have been a favorite among the kids."

"That's great."

"What would be even greater"—he nudged her shoulder—"is if someone would paint amazing landscapes on my pieces."

She snorted behind her cup.

"Picture it. A snowcapped mountain scene. Ocean waves below a stormy sky. You could go monochrome. Or retro. Modern? Youthful? The sky's the limit, Gwynn."

She refused to admit his vision was slowly winning over the creative in her. "You haven't seen my work to know if I'm any good."

One corner of his mouth quirked. "And you haven't been on social media lately or you'd have seen a new follower lurking and liking your posts."

She grinned. "You're a stalker now?"

"You're a worthy cause." His gaze held hers, warming her faster than the space heater.

Time had chiseled the boyish lines she'd loved so much into the hard planes of a man. Planes she could grow to love again. *But am I allowed to, Lord? You know my heart, my capabilities ... my* in*capabilities. Isn't it safer for me to remain detached considering my heritage and past?*

Yet she served a God who redeemed people's mistakes, creating masterpieces where one once saw junk. He could do that for her ... but maybe it hinged on her facing the truth surrounding *that night.*

Remember, Meister K had said. Did he know about her lost memories?

You comin' fer the ranch? Charlie had asked. *You gonna dig up the hidden money?* What did he know about that night?

Cash smoothed a gloved thumb across her puckered forehead. "Now would be a nice time to blurt out your inner thoughts. I like that habit of yours."

"A bad habit."

"Depends on where you're standing." He tugged one of her braids. "Though I can see how it might cause trouble working at the art gallery."

"Something I'll have to rectify when I return." *If I return.*

"Would you believe I forgot my spectacles?" a gravelly voice asked.

Gwynn spun on her heel. Gramps!

"What's a Santa without his spectacles?" he continued, shuffling around the counter in a lush, maroon Santa suit. A black belt encircled his waist, and a curly white wig sprung from beneath a bouncy Santa hat. He bent low, reached inside the top shelf, straightened again, and slipped on the glasses. Turning, he looked first to Cash and then to Gwynn. "Good?"

She angled her head away and took a slow sip of cocoa to hide her exposed face. At the same time, she wrestled with the instinct to throw her arms around the old man in a hug.

"Your beard's crooked," Cash said.

Gramps fiddled with it, and Gwynn sensed his curiosity. "Do I know you?" he asked.

"This is Gwynn Sadler." Cash put a hand at her back as if lending her courage. "She's out visiting the Davisons."

Gramps stilled. "Well, sear me in butter and call me a wall-eye!"

That brought her gaze to his.

His lips spread into a toothy smile. "I *knew* you weren't dead."

Gwynn lowered the cup, blinking back tears. "You did?"

He framed her cheeks in his white-gloved hands. "Had no reason to believe such a thing, mind you, but I couldn't shake it, even after all these years. With what happened to your family and all the not-knowing surrounding that night, I reckoned you had a reason to disappear."

"Keep your voice down, Gramps." Cash glanced at a group of teenagers walking past. "No one can know who she is."

"Then why is she back?"

"A misunderstanding brought me out here," Gwynn said, "and a snowstorm kept me here."

"The Lord, you say?" Gramps winked, and he looked like the quintessential Santa. "Your secret's safe with me, girl. Just press into the Lord. He knows what He's doing."

"Wish I could be as confident."

Gramps pulled her in for a hug and kissed her cheek, his synthetic beard prickling her skin. "I'm needed at the Santa Shack, but you swing by the workshop soon, you hear? We have lots to catch up on." With an exaggerated *ho, ho, ho*, he ambled from the shelter.

Cash blew out a breath. "Sorry about that."

Gwynn swiped at her eyes. Gramps recognized her—and he hadn't reacted in anger. Then she frowned. "Am I that recognizable?" She refitted her scarf over her nose and chin. "But Tessa didn't make the connection."

"She wasn't looking for you. Neither was I."

"Neither was Gramps."

Cash grunted. "Yeah, but … it's Gramps. He's the most perceptive guy I've ever met."

Press into the Lord. He knows what He's doing.

Gramps thought God had a hand in bringing—and keeping— her here. While she fully acknowledged God allowed it, what did that say about her attempts to return to Boston? Would she be working against His plan while trying to force her own?

Groaning, she let her head fall back. "You want me to stay, don't You?"

"Um … yes?" Cash said, a smile in his tone.

"I wasn't talking to you." She scrunched her face and heaved a sigh. "Fine. I'll stay. At least until I regain my memories."

Cash studied her. "Do I have God to thank for this sudden shift?"

"Blame or thank—it's a fine line at the moment." Her heart gave a painful lurch. "Irene. My job. This could be the final blow when I tell her I'm not coming back yet."

He rocked on his heels with a playful grin. "All the easier to convince you to work with me."

"Oh, good, you're here." Aunt Maude bustled into the shelter, gift bags dangling from her wrist. "My conversation with Ellen morphed into a bit of shopping and lasted so long, I was worried I wouldn't find you again. Are you ready? Penny Roberts is selling her delicious jams this year, and she's offering samples. I'm dying to try her cinnamon apple flavor." She looped her hand through Gwynn's arm and began to pull her away. "Will we see you at the dance this evening, Mr. Cooper?"

"Yes, ma'am. A phenomenal woman has promised me a dance." Cash winked, and Gwynn's stomach went all squirrelly.

Sticking around did have its upsides.

Chapter Twenty-Three

BY THE time Gwynn returned to the Jamboree after Aunt Maude's spaghetti dinner with her homemade secret sauce, tiny snowflakes drifted in the air, and mini white lights illuminated the rows of kiosks with a soft, magical glow. Adjacent to the peak-roofed gazebo, where couples twirled and swayed, a live band performed a mix of Christmas carols and golden oldies, their tunes carrying across the park.

A jumble of emotions knotted along her spine, pulling her in several directions, but anticipation won out as she rose on tiptoes and scanned the crowd for Cash. She could almost forget what had kept her from Prospect all these years … and what kept her from moving back even now.

Cash wove between a nearby circle of onlookers, his grin wide, his gaze admiring. "You look beautiful."

Gwynn smiled. She'd taken out her braids, reapplied her makeup, and left her scarf draped around her neck, trusting the evening's darkness would adequately shroud her face.

He took her by the hand, his warmth traveling up her arm, and led her to the gazebo. "I've waited all day for this. I hope you remember how to swing."

"That's one thing I didn't forget."

On the dance floor, with the band playing a jitterbug version of Let It Snow, she and Cash quickly fell into the routine of the basic swing steps, adding a few intermediate moves as they grew comfortable. They spun, they hustled, they dipped, and once, Cash even flipped her over his arm.

"Do you remember they used to hold a swing competition for the students?" Gwynn asked as they completed a round of complicated footwork. "We won that year you were a sophomore and I was in eighth grade."

"'Course I remember." He twirled her and resumed the basic rock step. "I was a hormonal teenager, calculating which moves gave me the excuse to hold you close." He spun her out then in again and pulled her against him. "I also remember you denied me a good night's kiss."

"We weren't dating yet."

"But then the following year ..." Cash dipped her with a sexy grin. "We ended the dance with a phenomenal make-out session."

Gwynn laughed as he drew her upright.

"If I recall, I strategically maneuvered us into a darkened alcove. Like this." He glided them toward a corner. "We slowed our pace despite the peppy music."

She looked away from his keen expression.

"You got shy, like you're doing now."

"Shut up."

"And I lifted your chin ..." With a knuckle, he raised her face to his. Her heart pounded against his chest as his thumb moved over her lips. "And I asked if I could kiss you. Again." He lowered his head, his eyes asking the question as his mouth hovered above hers.

Her lips parted, her eyelids drifted closed—

No! She ducked her head and pressed her free hand against his chest. "We can't. I don't want to mislead you into thinking there can be anything between us but friendship," she whispered. "What if I disappoint you?"

Cash sighed and dropped his hand. "You're like a song on perpetual repeat, the annoying kind no one wants stuck in their head."

"Thanks."

"Gwynn, we all disappoint people at times." He frowned. "But with you, it goes beyond that. There's a wall you've built up I can't break through, no matter what I try."

"It's not worth breaking."

"Why? Do you think you're not worth it?"

Her gaze hovered at his chin. "The proverb, 'the apple doesn't fall far from the tree,' exists for a reason."

"You're nothing like your parents. Hasn't the way you've lived these last nine years proven that?"

"Because I've gone out of my way to prove it wrong. I've been intentional. But when it comes to dating relationships, I prefer to watch them on the flat screen from the safety of my couch."

"Safety," Cash repeated on a murmur, smoothing a lock of hair from her cheek. "I wonder … did you worry you would hurt *them* or worry they would hurt *you*? Did you walk away first, or did you force them away before they glimpsed the real yo—" His hand tightened at her waist. "Doggone, that's what you did with me, isn't it? That's why you kissed Trent at that stupid Valentine's Day dance."

Gwynn lowered her gaze farther to his coat collar as the live band relaxed into the heart-stirring tunes of "I'll be Home for Christmas."

"Why push me away?" Cash asked. "I already knew the real you. I loved you. I wanted to marry you as soon as it was legal." He gave her a little shake. "You loved me too."

"I did. And it scared me." She curled her fingers into the folds of his coat. "You were the perfect son of perfect parents—"

"We weren't perfect."

"—Content to live the rest of your days in this town, when I simply wanted out of here. The accidental offspring of a world-class manipulator and his smarmy wife."

"I never saw you that way."

She forced herself to meet his gaze. "What if we had gotten married and I … I turned out to be like my mother—resentful and bitter, with a wandering eye? What if you turned out to regret your choice of a wife? I couldn't risk us hurting each other like that."

"So, you pretended to cheat on me?"

"Finding your girlfriend kissing another guy is less painful than catching your wife with another man. I was protecting you."

"You were protecting yourself." The muscles in his jaw popped. "You didn't trust that I loved you and was committed to making things work, despite the hardships."

The air rushed from her lungs. Was that true? Is that what she'd done? She rubbed at the pounding in her temple. "You deserve a nice girl from a stable family, Cash."

"What if *you* deserve a nice guy from a stable family?"

"A nice guy from the family I may have helped destroy?" Gwynn shuddered and retreated a step. "How could you want that? Want *me*?"

"Because I don't believe it. Please—" Cash gripped her arms before she could retreat farther. "Don't push me away again."

"But—"

"Do you care for me?"

When had she ever *not* cared for him? "Y-yes."

"Do you think you could come to love me again?"

She licked her lips and whispered, "Yes."

"Then stop fighting the inevitable, Gwynn, and trust me. Trust us." With a hesitant smile, Cash cupped her cheeks. "I'm going to kiss you now," he said, his voice husky. "And I hope you kiss me back." Her pulse raced as he inched closer.

"I thought I'd find you two hiding over here," someone said from behind Gwynn.

Cash groaned and rested his forehead against hers. "Later, Gramps. We're having a moment."

"Don't blame me for your dilly-dallying. If she were my girl, I'd have already put a ring on her finger." Gramps took her hand and placed it in the crook of his elbow. "Gwynn, darlin', it's time to humor this old geezer and take a turn with me about the dance floor."

Cash arched an eyebrow. "If you're dancing, who's manning the booth?"

"You. Better git to it." Gramps chortled, leading Gwynn away, and she threw Cash a rueful grin over her shoulder.

That kiss would have to wait.

After two lively songs, Gramps walked Gwynn back to the kiosk, but Cash wasn't there. Instead, a young woman sat at the checkout counter talking with a tall lanky fellow who wore a Montana Griz beanie and examined one of Gramps's Santa figurines. Gwynn's heart jackknifed, and she froze, her scarf laying limp and ineffective at her neck.

"Ah. Duke and Lainey." Gramps rubbed a hand over his mouth, his gaze flicking to Gwynn. "Do either of you know where we might find Cash?"

The young man replaced the figurine on the shelf among the other Santas. "Cash went to the barn with a customer who asked to see his other pieces. We don't expect him back for a while." He looked at Gwynn. "Who's this?"

Act natural. They might not recognize you. Forcing a smile, she held out a hand to her cousin. "Name's Gwynn Sadler."

"Duke Forrester." He shook her hand, his gaze sharpening. "Nice to meet you."

The woman slid from the stool and joined them. "I'm Lainey, his sister." She took Gwynn's hand and studied her face. "So, *you're* Gwynn. Tessa Reynolds mentioned you earlier."

"Oh?"

"She said she suspected ..." Lainey swallowed, her fingers tightening. "She said you might be Hadley Jacobs."

Gwynn's heart pounded in her ears. When had Tessa begun to suspect? Had Cash said something?

"You do resemble her ... kind of ..." Lainey's smile trembled, her expression hopeful.

Gwynn averted her gaze, the telltale sting of tears back in her eyes. If she lingered much longer, she'd cave and confess everything. *Lord, how do I get out of this?*

Or was she supposed to face it?

"Tessa's delusional, Lainey." Duke waved a hand at Gwynn. "Sure, there's a similarity, but Hadley is ..." His expression hardened. He crossed his arms and glared at Gwynn. "You know, that would be a cruel trick for her to play, pretending she's dead when all along she's been alive."

Gwynn's cheeks burned and her lungs constricted. She'd fled Prospect in a daze of horror and desperation, focused solely on herself ... yet she'd created a different horror for the loved ones she left behind. "I'm sorry, I didn't mean to make things awkward." She retreated from the pair.

"You didn't make it awkward." Lainey frowned at Duke. "My brother did. Don't leave on account of him."

"I need to get going, anyway. Nice to ... meet you both." She flashed Gramps a smile and hurried from the kiosk through the dwindling crowd toward the side street. That was too close.

"Gwynn, wait!"

She glanced back. Resigning herself to the confrontation, she let Lainey catch up to her.

"Forgive Duke's rudeness. We each dealt with Hadley's loss differently." Lainey's eyebrows drew together. "But … I can't let this go, and I'm sorry if *I'm* now the rude one, yet the resemblance—" She pressed her gloved hands together by her chin. "It is you, isn't it, Hads?"

Pinpricks of light danced at the edges of Gwynn's vision. "Lainey—"

"We had tea parties with our stuffed animals. Fed donuts to my dogs. Paraded around in Mom's too-big high heels." Lainey choked back a sob and drew Gwynn into a hug. "I know you," she whispered in Gwynn's ear. "Beyond the hair and colored contacts, I know it's you, Hadley."

A whoosh of memories assailed Gwynn in that hug. Yes, the tea parties and dress-ups, but also the board games and romps in the woods and myriad sleepovers. Anything that allowed Gwynn to escape her dysfunctional home life in favor of a sound one.

Gwynn gave Lainey a fierce squeeze, and tears leaked from her eyes. "Yes, it's me. I'm sorry for the deception, but it was necessary."

"*Why?*" Lainey pulled away and wiped her own tears. "I don't get it. I friggin' went to your *funeral*—"

"Shh." Gwynn dragged Lainey to a secluded spot behind a kiosk. "Look, I know you want—*deserve*—an explanation, but it's a long story. Can we meet up another time to chat? Maybe … Monday morning?" Since she wasn't flying back to Boston, she may as well fill her schedule. Less free time meant less time to ponder her life's current messy state.

"How about you come out to the farm?"

"No, your folks can't know about me yet." Gwynn glanced over her cousin's shoulder at the milling crowd. "The fewer people who know I'm alive, the safer it is for me right now."

"But Duke probably suspects. And Tessa—"

"They suspect, but they don't know for sure." Gwynn fisted the ends of her scarf. "I aim to keep it that way for as long as possible."

Chapter Twenty-Four

"I REALLY need to get your phone number," a voice rumbled near Gwynn's ear where she sat in the pew waiting for the church service to begin.

She looked up into Cash's handsome face, inches from hers as he stood in the aisle, leaning toward her. His dark, unruly waves flopped over his forehead and curled behind his ears, and his eyes sparkled from the sunlight streaming through the windows. Her heart tripped.

"If I'd had your number last night," Cash continued, "I could have let you know where I'd gone instead of letting you think I'd blown you off."

"It's okay," she said, her voice breathy. He made quite the picture in his all-black attire, from his wool coat down to his cowboy boots and the Stetson in his hands. His maroon scarf was the one splash of color. "I heard you'd gone to the shop with a potential customer, so no harm done." She scooted closer to Uncle Russ to let Cash join them in the pew.

"No harm done?" He slid beside her and teased, "I never got that kiss."

Gwynn fanned her flaming cheeks with the church bulletin she'd been reading. "What are you doing here?" She looked behind them toward the entrance, where two elderly couples lingered and chatted. "Is this your home church?" For the last few years, the Davisons had been driving the half hour into Livingston each Sunday to attend this small congregation. Gwynn thought she wouldn't be recognized, but if Cash had come all the way from Prospect … She whipped forward again. "Who else am I going to run into?"

"No one." Cash settled his hat on one knee and unbuttoned his coat. "Miss Maude may have let slip yesterday where she and Russ attend services … and that you'd likely be joining them." He winked. "Thought I'd check you—er, check it out for myself."

Gwynn smirked. "Way to be transparent."

"I have nothing to hide and a lot of time to make up for."

She elbowed him in the ribs. "How'd it go last night? Did the customer like your work?"

"He did. Name's Mark Hudson. He's here visiting family but wants to showcase several of my pieces in his furniture store in Miles City."

"That's wonderful! Congratulations."

Cash draped his arm along the pew behind her. "Now imagine if I had a partner who brought a whole new level of brilliance to my pieces with her painting."

Gwynn's nerves scrambled at his nearness, and she toyed with the bulletin, rolling it into a tube. "That would be quite the feat, considering your pieces are already brilliant."

"Ah, but her talent offers a unique perspective."

"She lives nearby, then?" Gwynn flattened the tube, pressing it against her thigh. "Or are you going to fly her out every time you want something painted?"

His thumb drew circles on her shoulder blade, and goose-bumps peppered her skin beneath her shirt sleeves. "I'm in the process of convincing her to move."

"You must work well together, for you to go to such lengths."

"We do have great chemistry."

With restless fingers, she mangled the top edge of the bulletin. "Sounds like a big risk to me."

"I serve a big God."

She stilled and looked at him. "You … you're praying about this?"

"You're surprised?"

Gwynn hmphed and crimped the bulletin in a fist. "Let me regain my memories before you and God unite against me. You might not like what I discover."

Cash's truck bounced over the rutted dirt road that cut through a narrow canyon outside the town limits. Gwynn clenched and unclenched her hands as she chewed on the inside of her cheek. Several new houses had sprung up between town and the AJ Ranch in the last decade. Life had pressed forward while a piece of her heart remained shuttered in the past.

A few minutes later, the mountains retreated and the land widened into a gradually sloping, snow-blanketed valley. Up ahead on the right, a massive log entrance came into view, and Cash turned off the road, steering his truck under the timber archway. An iron sign reading, *AJ Ranch*, hung at a crooked angle on the crossbeam.

"Someone's been here recently," Cash murmured, pointing to the set of tire tracks in the snowy driveway.

Gwynn's breathing accelerated, and she put a hand on her churning stomach. "I don't suppose anyone else in my family faked their death?"

Cash slowed the truck. "We don't have to do this, Gwynn. If it's too soon—"

"No. I need to remember. We need to know. And there's money to be found."

"It doesn't have to be today."

"My life has been on hold long enough. I just didn't realize it until I came back."

Cash pursed his lips, but Gwynn gestured for him to continue down the driveway, lined on one side by twisted cottonwood trees and a winding, partially frozen stream. "If someone's at the house, we'll explain the reason for our visit. Maybe they'll invite us in for a tour." Rotating in her seat, she glanced behind them at the mountains rising across the valley, a mixture of white snow and green pines. "I will admit one thing, though—I've missed this sight."

"God's handiwork on display for all to see."

Gwynn faced front again as the truck jostled over channels washed out from years of neglect. She gripped the dashboard. Through a copse of bare aspen trees three hundred feet ahead, she could make out a faded yellow ranch house and a rotting gambrel barn. Her lip curled. "Man's handiwork, on the other hand, leaves much to be desired."

As they drove closer, the derelict state grew more apparent. Wherever the snow had melted on the roof revealed crumbling shingles. The barn's roof, too, sported jagged holes and bowed in the center, and an outbuilding listed so far to the right, Gwynn wondered how it still stood. Weeds had died in autumn's frost after overwhelming the front yard and pushing their way through the wooden slats on the front porch. A second-story window had been smashed and another boarded up, and faded paint peeled on the siding.

Despite the fresh tire tracks, the place looked deserted.

Cash parked by the barn. The rotting ambiance wove its

tentacles from the house, along the driveway, and into the truck.

Gwynn shivered. "Home sweet ho—" She gasped and snapped around to stare at Cash, his own gaze fastened on the house. "I wasn't thinking! The last time you were here, your dad …" She slapped her forehead. "Here I am trying to remember a nightmare that you can't forget. I am so sorry. Let's turn back. I'll jog my memory a different way, or—"

"Gwynn, take it easy." Cash refocused on her, a steely look in his eyes. "I already prepared for this. While your life has been on hold, mine has been haunted, and I believe God wants to give us victory. I'll be darned if Satan steals that victory because we were cowards. We're here, the place seems abandoned, and I promised I'd stand by you, no matter what."

"But—"

"We're doing this." He hopped from the truck, jogged around, and opened her door.

"Stubborn man." Gwynn scowled at his outstretched hand. "I don't want you to *stand by me* out of obligation. That might not keep you from turning on me if we have to confront our ghosts. And I don't need your help getting out of a measly truck." Knocking his hand away, she climbed down—

Her feet slipped out from under her, and she landed on her backside in the wet snow.

Her mouth dropped. "*Seriously?*" She looked up at Cash, who struggled to hide a grin, and a laugh escaped her, dispelling the unease that hovered in the area. "I give up. I am appropriately humbled."

Cash pulled her to her feet, shut the passenger door, and braced his hands against the truck on either side of her. His spicy scent wafted over her, comforting and familiar.

"Let's get a few things straight," he murmured, his crystalline gaze pinning her to the spot. "I'm not doing anything out of obligation. I'm standing by you because you have a good heart. You've always had a good heart, no matter what name you answer to. Did I always believe that? No. Had our paths crossed five years ago, I suspect I would have reacted in anger and bitterness.

"But God's done tremendous healing inside me these last four years." Cash's expression smoothed into one of gratitude. "He cleared my haze of trauma and helped me think rationally again." Cash dipped his chin, bending close. "Things went awry the night my dad and your parents died, but I do not blame you. Got it?"

Emotion clogged her throat, so she simply nodded.

"Now, as to helping you from the truck, I told you before— it has nothing to do with a woman's capabilities. It's about honor and respect." Cash swept a lock of hair over her shoulder then skimmed his hand along her back to rest at her waist. "If you ask me, woman is the pinnacle of creation, and it's one of man's greatest pleasures to take care of his woman." He gently urged her closer. "I wish you'd let me honor you, without protesting. I wish you'd give me a second chance to cherish you."

The rejections that had been building on her tongue fizzled. She felt undeserving, yet Cash found her valuable. She was inadequate, yet Jesus gave her worth. Alex had labeled her a disappointment in the past, yet who was he to influence her in the present?

The blood in her veins did not dictate her decisions—her depth of faith in Jesus did that.

What a fool she'd been for letting her parents' behaviors and lies cast lengthy shadows over her life. She'd used them as excuses to hamper her ability to heal and mature. No more. The excuses stopped today.

Forgive me, Lord, for listening to the lies more than the truth. Help me reject the fears and honor You with my decisions going forward.

A lightness spread across her shoulders and down the length of her body. Resting a hand on Cash's chest, she whispered, "Okay," rose on her tiptoes, and softly touched her lips to his.

His eyebrows shot up, and his teeth flashed in a grin. Cupping the back of her neck, he slanted his lips across hers and captured her mouth in a proper kiss. His other arm wrapped around her waist, crushing her to him. Heat curled in her belly as something dormant awoke within her, an emotion she'd kept buried for almost ten years, and she yanked off a mitten to thread her fingers in his hair and deepen the kiss.

How she'd missed this man—her friend, her champion, her complement.

Too soon, they broke away, their breathing labored as though they'd completed a morning run. Cash kneaded her lower back through her peacoat. "Finally," he growled. "I can tackle a whole legion of ghosts after that kiss."

Gwynn trailed her fingertips along the scruff on his jaw. "Then let's get this over with before our courage fades or we're charged for making out on someone else's property."

"Good idea." Cash gave her one last sound kiss. "We can go make out at the Plane & Knotty, instead."

Chapter Twenty-Five

THE CLOSER they drew to Gwynn's childhood home, the heavier her legs became and the faster her heart raced. Here, evil had continued to fester over the years, even though its source had been removed by her parents' deaths. No one had returned to rout the residue with a thorough cleansing, and she wasn't about to volunteer.

She'd come here for one reason only.

They crossed the front porch, the floorboards creaking under their feet, and Cash grasped the doorknob. Gwynn gulped. But the knob didn't turn, nor did the paneled door budge when Cash pushed against it.

Her shoulders sagged, and she released a breath. "I don't know whether to be relieved or disappointed."

"There's still the back door."

She shivered. "You go check. I'll wait here."

Cash jogged off the porch and disappeared around the corner of the house. Rubbing her arms, Gwynn glanced about then moved over a few feet and peeked through the streaked glass window into the living room. Dust motes drifted across the weak sunbeams filtering into the house at this end of the open floor plan. The sofa, recliner, and coffee table sat in the same arrangement they had during her childhood, but a rolled-up sleeping bag slouched on the threadbare rug near the corner pellet stove. Had that been there ten years ago?

She frowned at the barricaded window on the other side of the door which would have given her a better view into the kitchen. With a crowbar, she might be able to pry off the plywood.

Cash came around the opposite side of the house, shaking his head. "Back door's locked too, and all the rear windows on the first floor have been boarded up."

"Dangit."

He squeezed her shoulder. "I'm sorry."

"This place creeps me out, yet I need to get inside." She jiggled the doorknob. "Did I *promise* I wouldn't break in if we found the doors locked?"

Cash chuckled then kissed her temple, took her hand, and tugged her from the porch. "C'mon. Let's go."

"Already?" She resisted his pace but let him lead her to the truck.

"What else can we do?"

"I don't know." She kicked at a mound of snow. "I thought I'd have a breakthrough coming here. Leaving without one seems like I've failed."

"We'll figure this out. Russ used to be a sheriff. Maybe he can pull some strings and get us inside. Legally."

Once again settled in the passenger seat, Gwynn stared at her side mirror as they drove away until the ranch's log entrance disappeared behind them. She sighed and pried off her mittens. "How am I supposed to remember what happened if the best place to trigger my memories is off limits? Why would God bring me back to Prospect if He's going to keep me blocked?"

Cash reached for her hand and laced his fingers between hers. "Maybe He had another reason in bringing you back."

She stared at their hands, linked together like puzzle pieces. "I have to return to Boston eventually, Cash."

"Sure, for closure. But you don't have to stay there."

"What if I want to stay? I know there are those who can't stand city life, but it's not the complete pits. For example, I'll have other opportunities for my painting." *Once my creativity starts flowing again.* "Plenty of things to do." *Distractions from my loneliness.* "My job might be nonexistent by the time I get back, but I could find work at another art gallery." *If Irene hasn't completely tarnished my reputation.* Gwynn rubbed at an ache behind her ear. "Do I leave the life I've cultivated there to start at ground zero all over again elsewhere?"

Cash cleared his throat. "You're right. I forget we've lived different lives for so long." He gave her a smile, though it didn't reach his eyes. "We may find we're not as compatible as we once were. Our current goals might not align." His thumb traced circles on her skin. "I suppose it's a matter of what we're willing to give up, what we want to keep, and if we can find common ground."

She shifted toward him, leaning her shoulder against the seat. "What's your goal for the rest of today?"

"Just today?"

"Just today."

The corner of his mouth lifted. "I'm heading back to the Plane & Knotty to work on a project. Want to come with me, or should I drop you off at the Davisons' first?"

Gwynn shook her head. "They'll either be full of questions about you and me, or wrangle me into another game of Canasta, and I'm too brain-weary for card games. I want to paint. I haven't held a brush in over a week." She had no clue what she'd create, but the act of painting would help diffuse her frustration.

"We have supplies at the workshop, though I can't vouch for their quality."

"All I need is something with bristles, acrylic paint, and a blank canvas."

"Will a scrap plank of wood do?"

Gwynn flexed the fingers of her free hand. "Perfect."

Cash parked his truck behind the workshop next to a staircase leading to a second-story entrance. He pointed upward. "My apartment."

"What about your dreams for building a log cabin in the woods?"

"Still my dream, but it'll mean more once I can enjoy it with a wife and kids."

She had once shared in his dreams, and the allure was great to reinsert herself … except, no. Regaining her memories had to come first.

He ushered her through the shop's back door which opened to a room as deep as the front showroom and spanning the width of the barn. Bright florescent light fixtures hung from the ceiling, and the earthy scent of sawdust mingled with the tang of varnish. A table saw, drill press, planer, and other power tools lined the back wall.

Sawyer scampered from a beanbag bed in the corner and frolicked to Cash's side, his tail thumping in greeting.

"Where have you two been all day?" Gramps asked, sitting with his back to them across the room at a grand, scroll top desk. A doorway to his right led to the showroom. "I can understand not wanting to make an appearance at church, but that was hours ago." He rotated in his chair, a block of wood in one hand and a whittling knife in the other, and peered over his reading glasses. "I trust you two behaved yourselves."

"Define 'behave.'" Cash winked at Gwynn before moving toward a scrap wood pile.

Gramps narrowed his eyes, but Gwynn held up a hand. "Cash was a perfect gentleman." One who presently evaded giving a straight answer, since "trespassing" didn't equate to "behaving." She crossed the room to Gramps. "What are you working on?"

"New snowmen for the shop, to replace the ones I sold on Saturday."

Cash withdrew a wooden board about one foot by two feet in size. "Will this do?"

She nodded.

"And what are *you* up to?" Gramps gestured around the room with his knife. "You gonna create with us like old times?"

"The creating part is questionable these days."

Cash motioned to the small table beside Sawyer's bed. "You can work there, if you want, or sketch on the floor with Sawyer, like you used to with Manny."

Gwynn smiled at the memory of Gramps's old Golden Retriever. "Sawyer seems to shed more than Manny. I'll go with the table."

They fell into companionable silence as Cash measured cuts on unfinished oak beams, Gramps whittled, and Gwynn … drummed her fingers on the table. What to paint, now that she had the opportunity and necessary supplies?

Her thoughts returned to the ranch house, and an involuntary shudder rippled through her. Its decrepit ambiance clashed with the one she'd painted in the landscape Meister K had bought. Time and separation had allowed her to imbue *that* imagined ranch with the joy and contentment she had longed to experience as a child.

Now the true image was too raw and recent for her to pretend away.

Gramps whistled the opening notes to an old hymn, drawing her attention. Shavings fell around him—on the desk, on the floor, on his shoes. His hair stood on end, like he'd gelled it and raked his hands through it from root to tip. His plastic-framed readers had slipped to the end of his nose, and he squinted at the rough, wooden form in his gnarled hands.

Gwynn's lips lifted. Though she struggled with proportions in lifelike portraits, she had a decent hand for caricatures, and Gramps made such a comical picture, how could she not seize this moment?

In a light pencil sketch on the wood surface, she captured his wild hair, the hunch of his back, and his tapping foot as he whistled. When she switched to paints, however, she focused first on the background, blending different colors on her pallet to match the rich mahogany tones in the scroll top desk. With a narrow brush, she brought to life the row of slim drawers along the interior's back wall and the deep cubbyholes crammed with letters, books, and pens. A little square door centered among the cubbyholes housed a small compartment—

Gwynn's brushstrokes slowed.

Gramps used to stash candy and other fun trinkets in that compartment, to the delight of little kids who visited the work-shop.

Paint pooled beneath her bristles as something slinked at the back of her mind like a murky shape obscured in haze.

A memory.

She grasped for it—but the shape disintegrated, leaving her feeling more bereft than before.

Shortly after midnight, after lying in bed for an hour and marking the moonlight's progression across the ceiling, Gwynn sat up with a gasp.

She knew where she'd hidden the money.

Chapter Twenty-Six

BUNDLED IN her peacoat, arms crossed against the single-digit temps, Gwynn trudged toward the The Nutty Bean on Monday morning to meet Lainey for coffee. Last night's revelation had given her yet another incentive to find a way inside the ranch house, but ever since, her stomach ricocheted in random directions like it was caught in a pinball arcade game.

The one thing she needed to do was the last thing she desired. What if she couldn't handle the truth?

The truth will set you free.

She adjusted the scarf covering her nose. Would it, though? Or would it send her to prison?

At least Cash would get his money.

"Provided no one's found it yet," she grumbled, approaching the coffee shop where Lainey stood, waving, beneath The Nutty Bean's swirly logo engraved on a wooden sign.

She greeted Lainey with a hug. "Of all the cafés in town, you had to choose this one. Hadley is the last person Tessa wants to see here. And what if Ainsley's working?" Gwynn couldn't keep her face covered and drink coffee at the same time.

"Tessa doesn't know for a fact you're Hadley, it's Ainsley's day off, and there *are* no other cafés." Lainey tucked her hand through Gwynn's arm and pulled her into the shop. Warm air and the rich scents of espresso and sugar greeted them.

Gwynn's body relaxed. Perhaps Tessa had mellowed over the years, and she'd now treat "Hadley" as courteously as she treated Gwynn.

She followed Lainey past a menagerie of beanbags, plush hassocks, and wrought iron tables and chairs to the counter near the back half of the shop. An electric fireplace graced one side wall, its mantelpiece adorned with delicate Christmas greenery and mini white lights. A massive painting of rambling cherry blossom branches hung above the fireplace.

Now *that* would look fantastic on one of Cash's pieces.

This place was getting cuter by the second.

"What about Chuck's Big Cup?" Gwynn asked, loosening her scarf.

"Went out of business. And Verdie's Vittles doesn't make coffee any better than they did ten years ago. Morning, Willow." Lainey smiled at the black-haired barista behind the counter. Sounds emitted through an archway off to the side, indicating others worked in a back room. "I'd like your peppermint mocha with whipped cream, please." Lainey tapped the small display case on the counter that held scones, muffins, and other pastries. "And one of those blueberry scones." She turned to Gwynn. "What would you like? This is on me."

"Oh, you don't need to—"

"My favorite cousin has come back from the dead, and I'm going to celebrate. Choose."

Willow's eyebrows arched, her finger poised over the register tablet.

Gwynn elbowed Lainey. "You make me sound like a walking zombie." To Willow, she said, "I'll take a white mocha. With a shot of butterscotch," she added, recalling the drinking chocolate from Saturday. "And a blueberry scone for me, too, please."

Willow nodded and quoted Lainey the price. Lainey propped her purse on the counter, removed her wallet, and counted out coins and paper bills.

Gwynn snorted. "If I'm a zombie, you're a dinosaur. Who uses cash these days, other than at the Christmas Jam?"

"I'm helping stave off full-fledged digital currency. If we don't use it, we lose it."

A dime and three pennies slipped through Lainey's fingers and pinged on the tiled floor.

Gwynn laughed. "You're losing it, all right." She chased after the bouncing coins, dropping below the countertop as a woman emerged from the back room.

"—don't know why you're not fighting for him," the woman said in a nasal voice.

"I don't have to fight. I simply have to bide my time."

Gwynn stilled where she crouched on the floor, her hand covering the dime. Tessa!

"Zeke swears Cash has fallen in love with her all over again," the other woman said.

"Like Zeke knows anything." Tessa scoffed amid sounds of shifting items. "Cash is looking for a way to jog Hadley's memory. He told me so on our lunch date. Said he has a new lead on where his family's money is hidden, and then he dished on how Gwynn is actually Hadley."

Gwynn's heart thumped as she gathered the pennies in her palm. She looked up and caught Lainey's wide-eyed stare.

"Can you believe she's been alive all these years? Living like a coward on the East Coast." Tessa's voice had turned snarky. Now *there* was the Tessa Gwynn remembered. "She's a means to his end, that's all. His opportunity to find the money. When she remembers where she hid it and confesses to Cash, he'll ditch her and—oh, Lainey! H-hi." A nervous giggle escaped her. "Have you been standing there this whole time?"

Gwynn rose to her feet. Behind Willow, Tessa and another woman were in the process of stocking shelves along the back wall. Tessa looked at Gwynn and red bloomed on her cheeks.

Gwynn forced a smile. "Good morning, Tessa. Cute place, The Nutty Bean, though I hear the coffee can sometimes come across as bitter." She cocked her head. "Or was that in reference to the management?" Dropping the coins in Lainey's hand, she met her cousin's gaze and jerked a thumb over her shoulder. "I'll wait for you by the fireplace."

It took two hours, two more scones, tears and a lot of laughter to catch each other up on a summarized version of their lives over the last nine years. Spoken in low voices so Tessa couldn't over-hear, of course.

"I'm so glad we got together," Lainey said as they exited the café, dabbing at her tears from their last round of laughs. She drew Gwynn into a hug. "And thanks for trusting me with your story. I won't say anything until you give me the go-ahead." Pulling back, she scowled. "Although with Tessa's loose tongue—"

"I know." Gwynn cinched her scarf around her neck, a gust of wind cutting through her flimsy peacoat. "My days of anonym-ity are coming to an end."

Lainey slipped her purse strap onto her shoulder and turned her scowl to the coffee shop. "I wish I could assure you of Cash's true feelings, but I only know what Tessa told me the other week before you showed up—that she and Cash were starting to get serious."

Gwynn's gut writhed, but she said, "It's fine, Lainey. It's not like he and I have an understanding."

"You're headed to his workshop now, right? Talk to him about it. You two never used to hide things from each other."

"Yeah, used to. We're not living in the 'used to' anymore." Gwynn batted the air between them. "Can we skip this topic? I had a blast hanging out with you—let's not ruin it."

Lainey grinned and retreated several steps. "I gotta run or I'll be late for my eye appointment, but keep me posted, okay?" She turned and hurried up the sidewalk.

Gwynn rotated on her heels in the opposite direction, toward Plane & Knotty Carpentry. She had a painting of Gramps to finish … and a possible confrontation with Cash.

He dished on how Gwynn is actually Hadley.

She's a means to his end.

When she remembers … he'll ditch her.

Gwynn clapped her mittened hands to her ears, but Tessa's words continued to clang in her head. Had Gwynn misread Cash to such an extent? When he looked at her … talked with her … when he'd held her at the dance … when he'd kissed her … he'd seemed genuine. Had he merely been leading her on? Did he still harbor resentment toward her, despite his insistence to the contrary?

Was he that good an actor?

She passed a box truck parked on the curb in front of the workshop, the Plane & Knotty's logo painted on its side. The large barn doors had been opened and anchored to the outside wall, and she stepped into a half-empty showroom. Cash and Gramps worked together sliding a tall, narrow dresser onto a dolly.

"What's going on?" she asked, tugging off her scarf.

Cash looked up and his expression brightened. "Hey, there."

Gramps grunted. "I see how it is, appearing when the work is done." He winked, dispelling any serious barb, and nodded at Cash. "I'll finish bringing this out to the truck."

Taking her hand, Cash led Gwynn to the back room where

they'd worked the evening before. "I was hoping to see you before I left. Still haven't gotten your phone number. I'm beginning to think you're purposely withholding it from me." He leaned back against the workbench and encircled her about the waist. His spicy scent followed.

She inhaled, plucking at a wooden button on his coat. How could she think rationally when standing this close to him? "You're leaving? Where to?"

"Miles City. Remember Mark Hudson, the one who's interested in my pieces? I'm bringing several to his shop today."

"That's a four-hour drive one way."

"Yeah." His thumbs moved up and down her lower back, sending fissures along her spine. "A high school buddy of mine lives there, so I'll stay with him overnight and return tomorrow."

She nodded, tracing the grain in his button with her fingernail. "That's cool."

Cash tucked a strand of hair behind her ear. "You okay? You seem … subdued."

"A little out of sorts, I suppose."

Cash is looking for a way to jog Hadley's memory. Tessa's words looped like a social media reel, but Gwynn couldn't just "talk to him about it," like Lainey suggested, when he was taking off in a few minutes.

"It's because I came across too eager and presumptuous yesterday, isn't it?" Cash asked. "I'm sorry. I was wrong to suggest you drop your current life in Boston simply because we reconnected. But I … care about you, and I don't want to watch you run away again."

"I'm not going to run away."

Cash cupped her face, a line forming between his eyebrows. "I don't want to watch you walk away, either. Or fly away. Or any kind of 'away.' God let our paths merge a second time, and at the risk of scaring you off"—he placed a tender kiss on her lips—"I'm praying He has more than friendship in mind for the two of us."

"And my memories?"

His brow knotted further. "What about them?"

"Shouldn't we wait until I remember what happened before we talk too much about the future?" She pulled from him to clear her head and straightened her peacoat. "I feel like I'm wandering around in a dream and can't wake up."

"You'll figure things out in time. Your mind has protected you for so long, it probably needs extra coaxing before it can relax."

When she remembers … he'll ditch her. "But what if it doesn't?"

Cash fisted a hand in his hair. "Why do you constantly look at things in a negative light? God wouldn't have brought you back without intending to give you closure from the past."

She quirked an eyebrow. "We never know God's true intentions until long after the fact. And even then, how often do we understand His reasons?"

"About to intrude," Gramps called from the front room. "Giving you fair warning in case you two are lip-locked." He chuckled. "I was young once, too, you know."

Cash pushed off from the workbench. "All clear, Gramps. Unfortunately," he added on a mutter as he passed her. Gramps entered and collected some paperwork from his desk while Cash grabbed his wallet and keys.

"I gotta get going. We can talk more later. Here." Cash unlocked his phone and handed it to her. "Add your number to my contacts. Service is spotty between Prospect and Miles City, but I'll call once I get settled."

"'Kay." Gwynn's fingers trembled as she created a new contact, blindly following the two men from the backroom, through the showroom, to the sidewalk outside. Tension had thickened between her and Cash like a can of old paint.

He checked the lock on the truck's roller door, and Gramps clapped him on the shoulder. "Drive safe. See you when you get back."

Gwynn returned his phone with a tight smile, and Cash bent down and kissed her. "Talk to you tonight."

"What if I regain my memories but we never find the money?" The words tumbled from her lips, and his jaw bunched, but she pressed further. "The love of that money killed my parents and your dad. Maybe we let it go."

Cash shook his head. "I won't accept that. It belonged to Dad, and he would've wanted his kids to benefit from it. My sister deserves to go to college."

"But—"

"Hadley, I need to get on the road. You'll remember, okay? Stop worrying." With a curt nod, Cash hopped into the truck and started the engine.

As he pulled away from the curb, she hugged her arms and whispered, "The name is Gwynn."

Chewing on her bottom lip, she walked back into the barn. Who or what did Cash care about? Gwynn in the present? Hadley from the past? Tessa? Or was his heart solely fixed on reclaiming that money?

She stared at Gramps's desk as the elderly man rummaged in the scrap bin by the corner, and her inner pinball game recommenced.

There was one way to find the answer.

Chapter Twenty-Seven

"MAY I borrow the car tomorrow?" Gwynn asked Aunt Maude as they washed the dinner dishes that night. "I won't need it for long. Maybe an hour or so?"

"I don't see why not. Russ? Do you need the car?"

Uncle Russ shook his head. "Where are you going? You want company?"

Gwynn opened her mouth to decline his offer but paused. She'd been planning to trespass on the ranch again; to pry off a loose board covering a window, and if that didn't work, then she'd try her hand at picking a lock. But what if whoever had made those tire tracks showed up, either before she arrived or while she was snooping around? Even if she armed herself with a gun for self-defense, she hadn't shot one since she'd fled Prospect.

She wrung the dish towel in her hands. Maybe Cash had a point and Uncle Russ could use his connections to help her. "I … I want to visit the AJ Ranch. I don't know how else to regain my memories"—and retrieve that money—"except go to the source where the madness occurred. But I'd be trespassing, so … how should I go about this?"

The Davisons exchanged a glance. Aunt Maude gave a slight nod, and Uncle Russ left the kitchen. Gwynn frowned. "What's going on?"

"Wait until Russ gets back. Here." Aunt Maude handed her a pot to dry.

A moment later, Uncle Russ returned holding a thick six-by-nine-inch manila envelope. He extended it to her.

Gwynn took the envelope and withdrew several sheets of paper and a set of house keys. Her gaze skimmed over the legalese, the words *trust* and *property* and *of age* jumping out at her. Her pulse thrummed. "What is this?"

Uncle Russ dried a serving bowl. "Together with Jeb and Edith, Maude and I bought the AJ Ranch after it went through probate. Got it for a song. No one wanted to touch it after what happened, not even that land developer, Neil Clifton. And since there was no lien on the property, the bank didn't need to inflate the price at auction." He tapped his finger on the papers. "We put it in a trust, to be held until your twenty-fifth birthday. Come mid-April, you'll be the ranch's legal owner."

Gwynn's world tipped for the second time in less than a week. She caught the edge of the island counter. "You bought the ranch? For me? Why would you waste your money like that?"

"It wasn't a waste," Aunt Maude snapped, slapping a wooden spoon in Uncle Russ's hand to dry.

Gwynn's face flamed. "I'm sorry. I don't mean to sound ungrateful, and I'm honored you thought of me, but—"

"Your father should've had a will," Uncle Russ said. "Had the courts known you were alive, the ranch would've gone to you eventually."

"Perhaps, although I was a minor at the time. In this case, you had to *pay* for it."

"We were happy to pay. You deserve an inheritance—"

"I do not." Gwynn paced away, the papers shaking in her hand. "I don't deserve any kindness you've given me. Not you, not Poppa Jeb or Mama Edith, not Cash, and should Uncle Erik and Aunt Dani forgive me for hiding away when they discover I'm alive, I won't deserve that, either."

"Sweetheart"—Uncle Russ gripped her shoulders and looked her in the eyes—"when are you going to forgive yourself?"

His words struck her like a physical punch. Forgive *herself*? She swallowed against the ache in her throat that appeared all too readily these days. "I-I can't," she whispered. "I'm alive yet my parents are dead. I enjoyed my do-over while friends and relatives mourned my supposed loss. I'm blessed with a deed to a ranch while others struggle to afford a simple studio apartment or a college tuition. How can I make amends for all of that? Why should I receive such favor when I don't deserve it?"

Uncle Russ let out a small sigh. "Why does God allow the things He allows? Why does He cause other things to happen? We don't know. We can't know, because we're finite beings with finite minds, incapable of seeing how God works all things together for good, according to His purposes." He gave her shoulders a little squeeze. "God has allowed you time to heal, and now He's brought you home. To face your past? Probably. To face your fears? Definitely. Everything else—everyone else—will fall into place."

Aunt Maude came over and swept Gwynn into a hug. "Time for you to stop feeling guilty about surviving, dearest," she murmured into Gwynn's hair. "The Scriptures tell us that those who have been forgiven much, love much, yes? Well, maybe those who have received much, bless much."

Gwynn cut the engine where she parked in the empty driveway

and clutched the steering wheel. Her childhood home waited beneath the overcast sky, its shadows taunting her with the secrets locked inside. She swallowed. Uncle Russ had again offered to join her, but she'd declined now that she knew she wasn't trespassing. Beyond that front door, she'd either have a mental breakthrough or a mental breakdown, and no one would witness it besides herself and God.

Which was why she'd ventured here before Cash returned from Miles City today. Not that she'd spoken to him since he left, even though he'd asked for her number. She glanced at her phone in the cup holder. More than twenty-four hours later, Gwynn worked hard not to read into his silence.

"Enough pussyfooting around," she said, unbuckling her seat belt. "Get in there and do what needs to be done." She pocketed her phone, grabbed her backpack purse and Uncle Russ's flashlight from the passenger seat, and exited the car.

Her heart pounded as she crossed the porch to the front door, the house keys jingling in her trembling fingers. On the second try, she fit the key into the lock and turned the knob. The door swung open to a dim interior, wan daylight seeping through the non-shuttered living room window.

The stench of stale cigarettes accosted her, and she paused, a chill stealing through her bones.

Her parents had done many things, but they'd never smoked. So, who had?

"H-hello?" she called. "Anybody here?" Had she been wrong to assume the house was empty?

When her question was met with continued silence, Gwynn crossed the threshold. She held the flashlight like a club in one hand and the keys in her other so that the jagged edges jutted between her fingers. With her elbow, she flicked the light switch near the door. Nothing happened.

"Okay, then." She rolled her shoulders. "We do this in the play of shadow and light."

Gwynn turned on the flashlight and passed the beam over the living room. The sleeping bag slumped in the same position as the other day. She relaxed and moved the beam across the dining area. The light caught on the beer cans littering the tabletop, and her muscles tensed again. In the kitchen, camping supplies and dishes cluttered the island countertop, and a ceramic ashtray overloaded with cigarette butts sat by the sink.

Her breathing accelerated. Someone was squatting in her house.

She slipped her hand into her coat pocket for her phone. Maybe she should have Uncle Russ join her, after all.

But as she retreated a step, the room spun and memories rushed at her with the force of ocean waves at high tide: Mother cooking at the stove, her blouses strategically placed to hide the black and purple bruises. Alex stomping in after a long day on the pretense of working a cattle ranch, disgust twisting his mouth, fists eager to release dark emotions. Mother sneaking into the house in the wee hours of the morning, reeking of another man's cologne. The constant, pervasive odor of whiskey and greasy food. Alex's impulsive backhanded cuff.

The images crashed upon the shore of Gwynn's mind, one swell after another, and she groped for the door handle behind her. Must. Flee.

No!

She blinked and shook her head to clear away the images. "You must stay, Gwynn," she said through gritted teeth. "This is what you've come for—memories."

How many would she have to battle until she recalled the ones from *that night*? And what would be left of her by the end?

"There's no way around, Sadler. You're going to have to walk through."

Straightening her spine, she dropped her hand from the doorknob and glared into the shadows where the past writhed like demons. "You're nothing but a vapor. Ugly to look at, yet no substance. You can't hurt me anymore." And her father was dead. He couldn't keep her bound in chains.

Unlock the memories and you unlock the chains.

The words sounded as clear as if they'd been uttered aloud.

"Unlock the memories … starting with the one I already possess." Raising her chin, she turned toward the closed door beyond the kitchen hutch leading to the staircase. What would her bedroom look like after sitting abandoned for almost a decade? Or had someone—perhaps this someone who smoked and drank cheap beer—already gone through her things looking for valuables?

Her heart thwacked. *Please let the money still be there.*

Hoisting her backpack higher on her shoulders, Gwynn hurried up the creaking stairs to the second floor and pushed open her bedroom door.

Chapter Twenty-Eight

SHE GLIMPSED the green paisley comforter on her twin bed before a tidal wave of flashbacks ambushed her, spinning and churning, cascading over her and leaving her sweat-drenched and gasping for breath. She had blocked the memories for so long, she couldn't bank them anymore.

"Don't fight it, Gwynn." She closed her eyes. "It's done. Finished. Let them wash over you and wash away again. They cannot harm you."

She opened one eye then the other and took a moment to calm her breathing. Outside, a ray of afternoon sunlight pierced through a slit in the clouds and filtered into her room.

Stuffed animals huddled on a chair in the far corner, wispy cobwebs traveling from toys to wall. A celebrity poster had fallen to the floor. Another poster clung to the wall, its top corner curling away from the dried-up sticky putty. Discarded clothes collected dust atop her bureau, and books had spilled from her wall shelf. Her comforter lay creased and wrinkled as though she hadn't finished making it. On her windowsill, a tiny glass Santa figurine winked at her, catching the last glimmer of light before the clouds eclipsed the sun again. Cash had given her the figurine for Christmas her freshman year of high school.

Everything looked the same in here—and yet everything had changed beyond these walls.

Gwynn turned to her secretary desk, a simpler version of Gramps' desk at the workshop sporting a drop front rather than a scroll top. He'd built it himself and given it to her on her thirteenth birthday. She extended the two support rails, lowered the front, and shone the flashlight inside.

Six cubbyholes filled with cards, notepads, and a collection of bookmarks marched across the interior back wall, three on each side of a center square compartment that boasted a little door. Much like Gramps's desk. But unlike his desk—Gwynn set down the flashlight and reached for the pair of two-inch-wide vertical columns flanking the square door—he'd made *hers* with a secret.

"I got it!" Alex exclaimed as he tromped through the front door. He held up a canvas sack the size of a shoebox. "That shifty Will Cooper thought he could keep this from me. Finding it on my *land—which means it's mine by right." He settled onto a chair at the dining table. "I oughtta skin his worthless hide."*

"You gave him permission to dig for artifacts while doing them post holes." Mother poured him a glass of his favorite whiskey.

"'Cause I didn't think he'd find anything! This changes everything."

It makes you a liar, *Hadley thought.*

Mother placed the whiskey on the table before Alex. "How much you think is there?"

"Don't know. It's gold nuggets and rolls of old bills—turn of the century, I reckon. Regardless of their face value, their age alone has gotta be worth tens, maybe hundreds, of thousands of dollars."

"Let's count 'em." Mother stretched a hand toward the bag.

Alex jerked it close to his body. "All in good time, woman. I ain't gonna jinx myself doin' it in front of the likes of you. A fella in Helena says he'll give me fair trade for the gold." Her father patted the canvas bag, looking at it with more reverence than he ever looked at his family. *"Just think how much wealth I'm holding right now."*

"What about Will Cooper? Won't he come after you?"

"I fired him. Can't have a money grubber for an employee, can I? Said I'd fire at him if he put so much as the tip of his nose over my property line."

"I like Mr. Cooper," Hadley blurted. *"What are he and his family supposed to do without—"*

"'I like Mr. Cooper,'" Alex mocked in a high-pitched voice. His lip curled. *"You like his holier-than-thou offspring, that's what you like."* He tossed back his whiskey in one swallow, eyes narrowing. *"You best remember where your loyalties lie, girlie, or I'll turn that hot-blooded stud into a gelding."*

Gwynn shuddered, her gaze snapping back to the present day, her fingers tightening on the vertical columns. "Thank you, God, for rescuing me from that man."

Now to undo the evil her father had wreaked.

She pushed the columns inward until a hidden mechanism *clicked.* They sprang forward, and she pulled them out, the columns mere facades to two narrow but deep drawers at their backs. Over the years, she'd hidden keepsakes or Christmas money she'd received from the Forresters, or …

Titling the drawers toward her, she released a laugh.

Or rolled up wads of stolen greenbacks and an old tobacco tin filled with gold nuggets.

She had crammed the drawers with the bills, wider than today's paper money and bound with twine, and they sat there still, untouched. *Thank you, Lord!*

Gwynn made quick work transferring the treasure to her backpack purse and returned the columns to their places beside the center compartment. Best to wait and examine the money in the safety of the Davisons' house. Would the value be enough to give Ainsley a chance at college or allow Cash to buy out Gramps?

Tires crunched on the gravel driveway.

She froze, the hair rising at her nape.

Shoot—had the squatter returned, or had Uncle Russ decided to join her? Slinging the backpack onto one shoulder, she hurried from the bedroom and tiptoed down the stairs. If she timed it right, she could escape through the mudroom before—

The front door banged open. "Show yourself!" a raspy, male voice called out. "I know someone's in here."

Her heart nosedived into her stomach, and Gwynn pressed her back against the stairwell wall, holding her breath.

"I see your car parked outside," the man continued. Boots clomped around the floor followed by sounds of shifting furniture and objects. "Come out with your hands up. I got a gun, and I ain't afraid to use it."

Icy fingertips slithered across her skin. *Lord, please help.*

But she would've had help, had she swallowed her pride and let Uncle Russ come along.

The man's boots made slow progress into the kitchen area. "Where you at? You skulkin' on the stairs?" A shot sounded, and the doorjamb splintered at the base of the stairs.

Gwynn yelped then cringed. Cover blown, she called, "Please don't shoot."

"Git out here."

Pulse racing, she raised her hands and stepped from the stairwell into the kitchen. Her eyes widened at the man in patched overalls, his pistol gripped in one hand and trained on her, a can of beer in the other. "Charlie Parker?"

"How do you know my—" He squinted at her, and his pistol trembled. The scar on his upper lip turned white. "It *is* you. Yer Hadley Jacobs, ain'tcha?"

She stared at the firearm and gulped. "Y-yes."

"You come back from the grave?" With an unsteady hand, he plunked the beer can on the edge of the kitchen counter. The can tipped and clattered to the floor. Dark liquid pooled around it. "You come to haunt me?"

Gwynn's pulse hammered an erratic pace. If he shot her, would her blood pool like the beer? "I'm not a ghost. I—"

"What're you doin' here?"

"It's my house. What are *you* doing here?"

The pistol shook harder, and Charlie clenched it in both hands. "I ain't no thief. I ain't goin' ta jail." His voice took on a desperate tone. "Alex said I was welcome to stay whenever. Gave me a key. And you ain't never come back—then you was buried. So, what're you here for now? You gonna kick me out? Toss me in the snow with all the other trash?" His nostrils flared, and he altered his hold on the pistol. "Hoity toities like you ain't got use fer trash."

She shifted on the linoleum floor, and the firearm followed. "Please, sir—"

"Don't you 'sir' me. And quit movin'. Think you can sweet-talk yer way outta this. You come and disturb a man's plans then act like it's *my* fault."

The man was talking in riddles. *What do I do, Lord?*

"Alex said he had a job fer me. Would tell me about it when I showed up. 'Cept I didn't make it. Got waylaid. So, I didn't kill 'em, see?" He swiped one palm on his pant leg, leaving a sweat smear. "I told them officers I had nuthin' to do with the murders, so you can— No. No, wait." His gaze darted about the kitchen, the pistol quivering in his hand. "Yeah, you just wait a cotton-pickin' minute. Yer here fer the hidden treasure." He looked back to her, his eyes narrowing. "I'm right, ain't I? Where is it? In the house?" He zeroed in on her backpack purse. "You got it in there?"

"I don't—"

"No more lies!" he screamed, his face contorting, flecks of spit gathering at the corners of his mouth. His fingers convulsed on the pistol as he retrained it on her, and Gwynn's throat closed. "You tell me where it is or—"

The pistol went off, the *crack* reverberating against the walls. Gwynn's knees buckled. Charlie swore and dropped the firearm, eyes flaring, head shaking.

"I didn't mean to! I didn't mean to!" he shrieked and fled the house.

Gwynn slumped forward as the scene from *that night* swallowed her.

Chapter Twenty-Nine

Nine years earlier, March

DRAPED ACROSS her bed, chin in hand and her dreaded geometry book open to the homework assignment, Hadley doodled flowers in the margins of her notebook with a gel pen. Flowers made way more sense than angles and degrees. Little navy-blue flowers … the same color as the jeans Cash had worn to school that day.

Scowling, she dug her pen harder. She shouldn't have noticed what he wore. And she wouldn't have, if she'd gone the long way around to math class after lunch. But she'd taken the shorter route, past Cash's locker, and of course he'd been there. So, of course she'd looked. And what hormonal teenage girl wouldn't have admired the way his favorite jeans hugged his thighs?

Yet the revulsion in his gaze … directed, for the first time ever, at herself—

The pen gouged a hole in the paper. Pretending she was into

Travis Phillips sucked, but she had to stick with it. Had to convince Cash she was over him. And when he graduated in a few months, he'd leave for college and find a new girl. Someone worthy of him.

A door slammed downstairs, and her father's outraged shouts rose from the living room. Hadley stilled her breathing.

"You're nothing but a stinkin' thief!" another male voice hollered, cutting off her father. "Where'd you stash my money?"

Mr. Cooper! Why was he—

Uh-oh. Hadley glanced at her desk then scrambled from her bedroom to the stairs. It shared a wall with the kitchen and hid her from view.

"You dare come into my home waving that pistol around?" Alex snarled as Hadley tiptoed down the steps. "Well, two can play at that game." Metal clicked. She grasped the railing. Alex must have reached for his revolver and cocked it.

"You stole my money," Mr. Cooper growled.

"It was found on my land. Makes it mine by right."

"You gave me permission."

"I take it back."

"Where's the money, Jacobs?" Malice coated Mr. Cooper's voice, and goosebumps peppered Hadley's arms.

"You ain't gonna see one dime of that money."

"Alex, let's think about this," Mother said, her padded footsteps nearing the other side of the wall.

Oh, no. Was she going for the hutch? Hadley fisted a hand in her shirt hem. If Mother looked for the money now—

"Vivian, don't you touch that money," Alex commanded.

A hutch door creaked open and items rustled. "You don't want people calling you a—oh! I-it's gone! The money's gone."

Hadley let out a whispered expletive.

"What do you mean, the money's gone?" Alex's boots stomped across the linoleum and objects crashed to the floor.

"Where'd it go?" he snarled. "You saw me put it in here the other day. Did you take it?"

"I didn't touch it."

"You stole it back, didn't you, Cooper?"

"Would I be here now, if I had?"

Slow and measured, her father's boots stalked back across the floor. "You're here to make me look the fool in front of my family. I'll show you who's the fool."

"No, Alex!" Mother shouted.

Hadley glanced around the doorjamb as her mother jumped in front of Mr. Cooper and Alex's revolver went off.

Mother's eyes grew wide, and she crumpled to the floor.

Hadley clamped a hand over her gasp and pulled back behind the wall, heart bucking in her chest. Bile surged in her throat.

"Now look what you made me do," Alex grumbled.

Yes, this is my fault, Hadley thought, a hand pressed to her roiling stomach. What had ever possessed her to hide the money?

Shouts erupted between the two men. If she didn't act fast, another person would end up dead. On silent feet, Hadley raced up the stairs and into her parents' bedroom. She yanked open the top drawer to her father's dresser and dug through his socks with quaking hands. One death on her conscience would haunt her forever. A second death—

No, Mr. Cooper would not die too.

Her knuckles scraped against a cold, solid object, and she snatched the Glock from its hiding place. She checked its clip, wiped her sweaty palms on her thighs, then slipped back down the stairs.

On the bottom step, she readied herself against the wall. *Please let all those afternoons learning to shoot with Mr. Cooper help me now,* she tossed heavenward.

Hadley stole another glance. Alex stood near the island counter, his Colt trained on Mr. Cooper crouched beside Mother as he drew a gloved hand over her eyes.

"I want my money!" Alex shouted.

"Vivian is dead, and all you care about is *money?* Go to hell, you bastard." Mr. Cooper whipped his pistol around and shot.

One of Mother's collectible plates exploded on the wall beyond Alex, and he flinched. Then his lips curled back to reveal gnashed teeth, and he took aim.

So did Hadley. She trained the Glock on her father's revolver and pulled the trigger as another shot reverberated in the kitchen.

Mr. Cooper jerked backward into the vintage pie safe.

Alex howled, dropped the Colt, and clutched his bloody hand to his chest.

Mr. Cooper slid to the floor, a dark red dot staining his coat front.

"No!" Hadley screamed.

She rushed forward, but Alex stepped in her path. "You ungrateful brat." He swung with his good hand, his fist connecting with her jaw, and the blow knocked her to her knees. "What the devil you think you're doing?"

Her vision swam and she tasted blood, but she held the gun in both hands and aimed it up at her father. "Stay away from me."

He swore and pressed his mangled hand against his body. "Think you're safe? 'Cause you got a gun and I don't? You ain't gonna use that on your old man." He advanced on her, and she scooted back on the cold linoleum.

"I said stay away!" Her voice shook along with her hands.

Alex spat on the floor. "C'mon, I dare yeh." She bumped into a corner, and he closed in. Blood ran down his forearm. Her finger froze on the trigger. "Yer nothin' but a useless, disappointing—" He spewed a repulsive word and lunged for her.

Movement blurred behind him. His mouth opened, and he made a strange sucking noise, his lips twisting as he dropped to his knees. He collapsed on top of her. She screamed. Her fingers jerked, and the Glock went off in his belly.

She clamped her eyes shut, her stomach revolting. She'd just killed her father.

Or had she?

Hadley tensed, anticipating his flying fists.

But Alex didn't move.

She opened one eye. A knife handle protruded from his back. She yelped and writhed beneath him, adrenaline tunneling into her arms as she heaved at his chest and rolled free.

The background came into focus. Mr. Cooper gazed bleakly at her, slumped against the base cabinets, a cutlery drawer opened nearby. Blood soaked his coat front, and his legs sprawled in front of him.

"Li'l Hadley Oakley," he wheezed. "You okay?"

"Mr. Cooper." Hadley crawled across the floor on trembling limbs to Cash's dad. "No, no, no." She flattened her hand against the wound in his chest. "I'm so sorry." Her voice broke on a sob. "This is all my fault. I … I took the money from Alex and hid it. I intended to get it back to you, but—" She glanced at her parents' lifeless bodies. Tears dripped from her chin. "But it got all messed up, and now it's too late."

A car door slammed outside, and she stiffened, her face going cold. She couldn't let anyone find her like this.

Get out get out get out!

Mr. Cooper's eyes had closed, and a fresh wave of tears seared her cheeks. "You saved my life. I'll never forget that. Never forget you." She kissed his forehead then hurried to the front door, flung it open—

She plowed into Cash.

Fool! Why hadn't she used the mudroom? What was Cash even doing here? She tried to flee past him, but he caught her arm.

"Hadley?" His gaze swept over her, and his eyebrows knotted. "Why is there blood on your—Are you hurt? What happened?"

She struggled against his hold. "It's my f-fault," she choked out. "I'm s-sorry." A useless apology. She was a monster.

"What do you mean, your fault?" Cash's hand tightened on her arm. "What's going on?"

"Please forgi-give me." She clawed at his fingers. "L-let me go. I need to—"

"Cash?"

Cash whirled at Mr. Cooper's hoarse voice. "Dad?" His hold slackened. She broke free and bolted down the steps.

She didn't stop running until exhaustion claimed her hours later on the snow-riddled forest floor.

Chapter Thirty

"GWYNN? YOU in there?"

That voice. It tasted like honey. Soft. Golden. Compelling. It tugged at her, pulling her from a bed of pine needles and ice.

Something whumped in the distance.

"Gwynn!"

Footfalls thudded closer. Calloused fingers caressed her cheek, smoothed her hair, clasped her shoulder. "Gwynn, wake up. Are you okay? Please, God, let her be okay."

Her eyes fluttered open. The forest dissolved into kitchen cupboards. Dim lighting seeped in from a window, and blurry jean-clad legs knelt beside her. She frowned, sprawled on her stomach on a hard, cold surface. "What's going on?" she croaked.

The fresh memories of that horrific night smashed into her then, stabbing her with a conflicted mix of grief and solace. She cried out and rolled to her side, curling into a ball.

How foolish she'd been! Her poor choices and rash behavior from the past had indirectly resulted in *three* deaths. She might not go to prison, but would her conscience ever be free?

"What's the matter?" Cash rested his hand at her waist. "Talk to me. Are you hurt?"

"It's true—it's my fault." She moaned and pressed her cheek into the linoleum floor. *Lord, forgive me.* "If I'd left the money alone, they might be alive today."

"I don't understand," Cash said. "Did you—"

"Yes, I found the treasure. You happy now?"

"That's not what I ..." He fell silent, and her shuddered breaths filled the gap. "So, you remembered. And you were here by yourself?" His fingers tightened on her waist. "I'm sorry. I should have been here with you. You should have waited for me."

She opened her eyes and glared at him. "You ghosted me. If Tessa's to be believed, I bet you didn't even have plans to call me." Pushing his hand away, she struggled to a sitting position. "Admit it—you've been using me. Tessa said—"

"Whoa, hang on." Cash took her shoulders and leveled his gaze with hers. "I didn't ghost you. You gave me the wrong number. Nine digits instead of ten. I tried calling the Davisons, but all I got was a busy signal, and then ..." He sighed and shook his head, rocking back on his heels in his crouched position. "Never mind. We'll discuss it later." He looked around. "What happened *here?* That guy told me you were in trouble—" His eyes widened at the floor by the island counter.

"What guy?" She spliced a hand through her hair, working to untangle her recent memories from the iron grip of the old ones. "I came here to get the treasure. Well, hoped to get the treasure. I remembered the other night where I'd hidden it and—"

"Who had the gun?"

"What?"

Cash pointed to a pistol on the linoleum floor. "Who had the gun?" He turned back to her, his brow pinched. "Gwynn, what the heck happened?"

"I-it was Charlie." Her body trembled. "He's been living here for who knows how long—claims Alex gave him a key—and he came back before I had a chance to—"

"Did he shoot you?"

"Well, the gun went off, but I think it was an accident—"

"Tarnation, woman, I asked if you were hurt." Cash yanked her coat open, his gaze raking over her shirt.

"Easy, Cooper. I don't *feel* hurt." She patted her torso. "And I'm not bleeding." Her palm grazed a scratchy spot near her coat pocket. "What's that?" She peered down and fingered the discolored area. A solid object had lodged into her coat material. Frowning, she worked it free, and a hard, misshapen lump about the size of a marble fell into her palm, leaving behind a frayed hole in her pocket. "What …?" She fingered the lump, her frown deepening. "Is this lead? What is this?"

Cash plucked it from her hand, and he blanched. "It's a bullet."

Her gaze met his. "So, I did get hit?" She flapped open her coat to check her hip and something thunked onto the floor. "My phone." She picked it up, the screen cracked like webbing around an epicenter where the bullet must have struck. She pressed the side button, but the phone was dead. "It stopped the bullet. Is that even possible?"

Cash compressed his lips, rolling the bullet between his fingers as sirens sounded in the distance. "I've heard of a few cases where it's happened, but not always. This is a miracle."

She worked to restrain the tears in her throat. "But why? Why is *my* life spared? Our parents are gone, and I'm to blame."

"Gwynn—"

"No. I remember everything, okay? It's my fault." Her eyes grew hot. As the sirens intensified, she told him about the exchange between their fathers, Mother inserting herself between the men, her own attempt to intervene, and Mr. Cooper stabbing Alex to save her life. "Do you get it now? If I hadn't hidden the money—"

"You can't blame yourself for other people's bad choices. So you hid the money. You didn't know what would come of that. And not everything ended badly." Moisture glistened in Cash's eyes. "You're still alive."

She swiped at her own tears. "And I'm grateful. But I'm a nobody. Why would God spare—"

"Knock it off, Gwynn." Cash cupped her chin in a gruff hold, a fire in his ice-blue eyes. "God doesn't make nobodies. You've got to stop asking 'why,' and start asking 'what.' And forgive yourself already. God clearly has more work for you to do, but you can't do it wallowing in self-pity and remorse."

Her mouth fell open. "I … I …" The protest to his rebuke fizzled on her tongue. He spoke the truth, dang it.

Boots clomped on the front porch. Two police officers burst into the house, followed by two EMTs and Uncle Russ.

"We were told there was a shooting," one officer said.

The female EMT nudged Cash aside and crouched next to Gwynn. "Where are you hurt, ma'am?"

"I'm not—"

"Let me through! Gwynn!" Uncle Russ pushed his way to the front, deep lines etched in his forehead.

"It's okay." Gwynn looked from her uncle to the EMT. "I'm all right."

Uncle Russ sagged against the counter and dug the heels of his palms into his eyes. "Thank you, Jesus."

One officer moved into the living room, talking into the two-way radio clipped to his vest. The EMT produced a blood pressure cuff from her bag and strapped it around Gwynn's arm.

Gwynn frowned up at Uncle Russ. "What are you all doing here?"

"I was listening on the transmitter when the call went out," he answered as the cuff tightened. "Apparently, Charlie Parker went to the station and confessed everything. Scared out of my mind he'd killed you." Uncle Russ hitched his chin at Cash. "What're you doing here?"

"Charlie told him where I was," Gwynn said.

"No, he didn't," Cash said. "I haven't seen Charlie since the Christmas Jam."

She cocked her head. "Then how'd you know where to find me?"

Cash ran a hand over his five o'clock shadow. "It's an interesting story, actually." His lips quirked. "One that's best shared over coffee and a slice of Miss Maude's award-winning huckleberry pie."

Chapter Thirty-One

SLOUCHING LOWER on the couch cushions, Gwynn pinched the lead bullet between her fingers and studied its deformed edges.

This is a miracle.

God has more work for you to do.

Laughter drifted from the foyer as Uncle Russ and Aunt Maude saw Sheriff Lee to the door. Across the room, the Christmas tree lights twinkled merrily, and Aunt Maude's Santa Claus wore his perpetual cheery expression.

Gwynn should radiate just as much cheer. God had spared her life—not once, but twice now—in her old house. So why did she, instead, feel like she'd been baked in Holly's kiln, dashed against a wall, then glued back together?

Stop asking "why," and start asking "what."

Ugh, and when would Cash's words quit playing in her head like an ad that kept popping up online?

Now that her memories had filled in the missing gaps and rounded out the police report, the cold case of her parents' and

Mr. Cooper's murders would officially close. No unknown killer roamed free, and Charlie no longer needed to fear the cops' suspicions.

Not all issues had been resolved, however. Fisting the bullet, she glanced at the canvas bag on the floor by her feet that held the recovered treasure. Where did things stand between her and Cash? Had he meant what he'd said to Tessa—and did it matter anymore? If either of them owed the other an apology, it was Gwynn for the part she now knew she'd played in Mr. Cooper's death. Would Cash forgive her?

And what about that odd Meister K, who had asked her to remain in Prospect until he delivered some kind of letter? He'd said that five days ago. What happened to getting it to her "in another day or so"?

She let her head fall back as Brisket barked in the central hallway. So many questions. So few answers. But God couldn't possibly expect her to hang around until they were all answered. Tickets for her flight to Boston already waited in her email, and she counted the hours until she returned to her normal life.

Or was she taking the coward's way out?

She groaned and draped her arms over her eyes.

Gwynn had faced down her nightmares, but she hadn't faced her dreams. She'd set those aside long ago and feared to reexamine them now. If she didn't let herself hope, she wouldn't be disappointed when they didn't come true.

"What do I do, Lord? Return to Boston, or stay here? Or is there a third choice I don't even know about?"

"If you're taking a vote, I'd like to weigh in."

Just as it had done in the airport last week, the smooth baritone slipped over her collar on a delightful shiver. Gwynn opened her eyes. "Eavesdropping again, Cooper?"

Cash propped a shoulder against the living room doorjamb, his barn jacket open over a charcoal gray fisherman's sweater, his eyes like the light blue horizon on a cloudless day, popping beneath his Stetson. A playful grin flitted across his mouth. "I learn a lot that way."

She sat up and repositioned herself on the couch as he approached. "If you're here for the pie, you're out of luck. Sheriff Lee ate the last slice."

His grin broadened. "I accept rain checks." He settled on the cushion beside her and removed his hat. "Actually, I spoke with the sheriff as he was getting into his car. He said you weren't pressing charges against Charlie."

"You probably think I'm crazy, but enough people's lives have been damaged because of what happened years ago." She rolled the bullet between her palms. "I didn't want to add to the pile. So, I decided as long as the authorities revoke Charlie's gun license, and he receives help from a community shelter in one of the nearby cities …" She lifted a shoulder.

Cash stretched forward and placed his hat on the coffee table. "I may not have done the same thing were I in your shoes, but knowing the hardships in Charlie's past, I can understand your reasoning." He braced his elbows on his knees and steepled his fingers. "And while we're on the topic of reason, I'd like to set the record straight with what you apparently overheard at The Nutty Bean."

"You don't have to. I've been thinking, and—"

"You said something yesterday about me using you, and 'believing Tessa,' so I went to confront her." Cash rubbed his hands along his thighs. "She admitted she exaggerated the truth when talking with her coworker, trying to 'manifest' her own reality or whatever."

"Okay," Gwynn said slowly. She pressed the bullet into her palm, its rough edge digging into her skin. "But how does she exaggerate a 'means to an end'? Or that I'm your 'opportunity to find the money'? You even told me yourself, before you knew I was Hadley, that you'd been searching for the treasure for a while."

"I never intended to use you to find it. It's true that during the … uh"—his ears turned pink, and he stared past her at the fireplace—"lunch date with Tessa last week, we talked about the promise I'd made my dad regarding the lost money. But you had just apologized to me, and that threw everything off-balance."

Cash drilled a hand through his hair, his curls flopping in disarray. "Suddenly, I wanted the chance to rekindle my friendship with you—and maybe more, if it were possible. I couldn't admit that out loud, though. Not only would I have sounded insane— emotions couldn't change that fast, could they?—but I knew how Tessa felt about me, and I … didn't want to be a complete jerk. In my attempt not to say too much, however, I ended up saying the wrong things. Tessa misunderstood me and ran with it."

Gwynn doodled an imaginary design on the couch cushion with the bullet, her hopes rising with his words. Then they dipped. "Right before you left for Miles City, you were so confident I'd remember what happened that it made me wonder which you were more interested in—me or my memories. And then you called me—"

"Hadley. I know." He grimaced. "I wish I could take it all back. Flippant words I never should've said."

"Out of the overflow of the heart, the mouth speaks," Gwynn said.

Cash scowled. "Out of distraction and impatience, the mouth speaks, as well."

She stared at the faint lines she'd created in the couch. *And out of desperation, one can act with just as much flippancy.*

"What do you mean?"

She snorted. Of *course*, she'd said that out loud. "Meaning"— Gwynn tossed the bullet at the coffee table, and it landed in Cash's hat brim—"so much has happened since your lunch date with

Tessa that it would be wrong of me to hold a few careless words against you. Especially when you now know the truth of how your father died—"

"I don't blame you for that."

"—so please forgive my reckless behavior that night." She bent over and lifted the canvas bag by its straps. "And may this compensate for my mistakes, although it rightfully belongs to you anyway."

She placed the bag on his lap. Slanting her a wary look, he untied the straps then peered inside at the money and tin she'd transferred from her backpack this morning. His face went ashen.

Silence sank between them like a sodden wool blanket.

"I don't blame you for what happened, Gwynn," he murmured at last. A muscle pulsed in his jaw. "I suspected what Dad was about when he left for your house that night. He's the other reason I went to the ranch." Cash closed his eyes. "But I was too late." Clearing his throat, he straightened and plopped the tote bag in her lap. "I can't take this."

"Well, I don't want it." Gwynn wrinkled her nose and pushed the bag to the floor. A *plink* sounded from the tin as the bag listed onto its side. "Reliving how greed and the love of money corrupted otherwise sane people ..." Her body convulsed involuntarily. "No, thank you." She toed the bag with her foot. "What a pair we make. Given the age of those bills, they might be worth hundreds of thousands of dollars. When you include the gold nuggets—"

"That money ruined our past. I won't let it ruin our future."

Several bills fanned out at the bag's opening. A piece of twine around one roll must have come untied from the manhandling and transfers from drawer to backpack to canvas bag. Gwynn angled her head.

That wasn't a fancy, turn-of-the-century profile of a smirking Ben Franklin.

Cash shifted on the couch. "Our future is what I want to—"

She grabbed his knee, her chest tightening. "Cash." His name came out strangled. "Look." With shaky hands, she reached for the old paper money, which began to flake apart in her fingers. Not the pile of greenbacks she'd expected.

They were greybacks.

Cash leaned close and whispered, "Confederate States of America?"

Chapter Thirty-Two

"IS THIS a joke? Some sort of nasty trick?" Gwynn lifted the bag onto her lap and pulled out another wide, rolled-up wad of money. She slipped the twine free. The bills unfurled to reveal a large-size 1923 US one-hundred-dollar bill rolled around a stack of deteriorating Confederate paper currency. "Is Confederate money even worth anything anymore?"

"Not in that state, it's not." Cash untied two more wads, each arranged in the same layout—an antiquated US bill wrapped about several Confederate bills, most of them in poor condition.

Gwynn's stomach threatened to eject her lunch. "Who did this? Who took the time to conceal defunct currency and then bury it?"

"Details lost to history, unfortunately."

She picked up a flaking bill. "Our parents died over someone's warped idea of a joke!"

"No." Cash kneaded his neck, his eyes pained. "You said it yourself—they died over the love and greed of money."

Gwynn popped open the lid to the palm-sized tobacco tin. A moan escaped her. "No handful of gold nuggets. Just one nugget and a smattering of gold flakes."

Cash took the nugget and held it to the light. He sighed. "It's pyrite. Fool's gold."

"How do you know?"

He looked at her, eyebrows rising. "We live in an old mining town, Gwynn. Our teachers drilled into us how to discern the differences between real gold and fool's gold."

"And yet our fathers didn't see it."

"People see what they want to see sometimes."

"You sound like Aunt Maude." She threw the tin back into the bag. "Unbelievable. Our parents died for nothing. You, yourself, wasted countless hours searching for *nothing*." She stood and paced in front of the fireplace. "If only I'd examined the 'treasure' for myself years ago, I wouldn't have been duped. Or if your dad had inspected it when he first found it on our land, he would've tossed it back in the ground. Then Alex wouldn't have had anything to steal and—"

"Gwynn."

Cash's soft tone drew her gaze. His Adam's apple bobbed once. "We can't play that game. It'll drive us mad. It's what I did after you disappeared years ago. If only I'd arrived sooner. If only I hadn't let you run off. If only I'd tried to stop Dad before he left. It won't help our situation."

"But this is stupid." She gestured to the bills splayed on the cushion. "Almost all of those bills—useless. Worthless."

"We don't know that for sure."

"I wanted to return your treasure, but all I did was get your hopes up." Discouragement built in her chest as she lowered herself to the couch again. "You're still a struggling craftsman, and Ainsley won't get her chance at college."

Cash placed the money and twine back into the bag. "God provides. And He'll help me figure things out with Ainsley."

Gwynn pushed against the ache behind her breastbone. "Why aren't you upset about this?"

"Not a day goes by when I don't wish my folks were alive, but I'm not upset about the money. I'd decided before coming here that I wouldn't accept it, even if you tried to force it on me, so I'm no worse off than I was an hour ago."

"But *I* am." She took a shallow breath. "My heart feels like a ship caught in a storm, first wrenched one way, then wrenched another … I'm about to capsize."

Cash framed her face, his gaze rock steady. "Then let God take the wheel, Gwynn. And let me help you man the sails." His thumbs moved over her cheeks, and he gave her a small smile. Standing, he reached for his hat and tipped the bullet from his brim into his hand. "You want this?"

She shook her head.

He pocketed it and tugged her to her feet. "C'mon, let's go for a walk. We could use some fresh air … and a fresh perspective."

They walked in silence, the sun shining in the brilliant blue sky even as tiny snowflakes floated lazily about them. The crusted snow glistened across front yards and evergreen trees, a sparkling contrast to the wrestling match going on inside Gwynn. Judging by the tic in Cash's jaw, he did his own wrestling.

Their meandering brought them to Bentley Park, and Gwynn sank onto a belt swing. The cold seeped through her jeans. Lifting her face to the sunlight, she inhaled. "Alex used to say that when our insides feel lousy, beautiful days are like a slap in the face."

Cash relaxed against the crossbar of the swing set's metal A-frame. "I say they're God's way of giving us a hug when we need it the most."

Gripping the swing's chains, Gwynn rotated toward Cash.

"That's what I always appreciated—and envied—about you. Your ability to see the silver lining in almost anything. To bring out the charm in a knotty piece of pine." She pushed away in a slow arc. "Or recognize the masterpiece beneath the scribble."

His lips twitched. "The way God works, I'm guessing scribbles are part of the masterpiece." He patted his coat and withdrew a red envelope from an inside pocket. "Speaking of scribbling, I was planning to give this to you earlier, before the whole money debacle."

She walked the swing closer to him. "What is it?"

"A letter." Cash passed it to her.

Santa Claus ~ North Pole was scrawled across the envelope in teenage penmanship.

Her teenage penmanship.

She sucked in a breath. "Where'd you get this?"

"'Member I had a story to tell you? I got a flat tire on my way home from Miles City. The company truck didn't have a spare, so I was stuck in the canyon with no cell service, wondering what to do next when a jolly old man in a 1940s Ford pickup came along and helped me." Cash flipped up his coat collar. "I think."

"You *think* he helped you?" Gwynn turned over the envelope. Its seal was broken.

"Well, I don't recall him changing my tire, but before he arrived, it was flat, and before he left … it wasn't." Cash frowned at the ground. "He wore a red and black plaid coat, so I reckon he's that same Santa-dude from before."

"You saw Meister K!" He'd gotten the letter to her, after all.

"Is that what we're calling him now? Anyway, we had the most topsy-turvy conversation. He's the one who told me I'd find you at the ranch. Said you might be in trouble."

She looked up. "How could he have known that?"

Cash shrugged. "He handed me the envelope and instructed me to give it to you. Apparently, he was supposed to deliver it himself, but 'it's crunch-time at the Workshop.' When I tried to coax further information from him, he said, 'Life doesn't wait for pokey boyfriends, and Christmas doesn't wait for Santa.'" Cash folded his arms. "Are you following any of this? Do you know what he's talking about?"

"Kinda? But you wouldn't believe me if I told you. I'm not even sure *I'd* believe me." Gwynn stood and walked over to the dome-shaped steel jungle gym as she took two folded sheets of paper from the envelope, one yellowed and old, one crisp and new. She unfolded the old one first.

It was the letter she'd written to Gramps almost a decade ago.

How had Meister K gotten his hands on this?

She climbed onto a horizontal bar and read her young words, several key lines jumping out at her.

Cash is an amazing guy and comes from an amazing family, and he deserves to be with an amazing girl.

He thinks <u>I'm</u> that girl, but deep down, I know I'm not.

… the truth of who I am, <u>what</u> I am, would only end up staining the unblemished canvas of his life.

This is where you come in … All I want for Christmas is for you to help Cash find a new girl. One worthy of his love, one he won't regret having chosen when he's old and gray …

Gwynn blinked away her blurred vision. What a lost soul she'd been—and still was in many ways, for hadn't she prayed along similar lines just the other day?

"Forgive me," she whispered, "for demeaning myself when I'm Your unique creation."

Shifting on the jungle gym, she unfolded the second piece of paper, a half sheet written in swirly handwriting.

> *Dear Gwynn,*
> *I trust you see now why I've taken so long to answer*
> *your letter (apologies for having misplaced it the other*

day!). In my defense, you never set a target date, and neither of you were ready until recently for the level of commitment marriage requires. But you have always been the "amazing girl" for Cash. If we had to prove ourselves worthy of another's heart before earning their love, I suspect the human race would have died out long ago.

I also trust your memories have been released, and you're in the beginning stages of healing. Therefore, my Christmas wish for you is that you'll leave your teenage burdens in the past and not allow your fears of the future to overshadow the present. I know too many lives shriveled by regret, a prayer on their tongues that they'd done things differently.

So, take risks. Fail. Get back up and try again.

Fall in love. Have quarrels. Forgive and receive forgiveness.

Rinse and repeat, as they say. ;)

May you be blessed, my dear girl, and may you be a blessing.

Merry CHRISTmas,

Santa

Gwynn swiped a tear, letting the words soak into her soul. Had the Lord inspired him? There was freedom in his words. Freedom to live. Freedom to have adventures. Freedom from fear.

For God did not give us a spirit of timidity, but a spirit of power, of love, and of self-discipline, Scripture said.

For we are God's handiwork, created in Christ Jesus to do good works. There is now no condemnation for those who are in Christ Jesus.

No condemnation.

Freedom.

Cash came to stand before her, propping one boot beside hers on the lowest bar. He nudged her knee with his. "You okay?"

Smiling, she dabbed at her eyes before her lashes froze. "God is good."

"Amen to that."

"No, really." She stuffed the letters back into the envelope. "Despite everything I've learned and remembered this past week, despite the things that look messy and feel unpleasant, I can take comfort in the promise that God is in control of it all. And He only ever operates out of His goodness."

She tucked her hands holding the envelope between her knees and gazed at the snow-covered mountains rising in the distance. "God's not petty or mean or manipulative. He's compassionate and merciful, slow to anger, abounding in love and faithfulness, and forgiving wickedness, rebellion, and sin. His ways are just. He's our refuge and strength, an ever-present help in times of trouble." A smile spread across her lips, her spirit encouraged by the beautiful qualities she'd rattled off.

Cash put a hand to his chest. "A woman who knows her Scriptures, be still my heart. Now *she* is worth far more than rubies."

Gwynn ducked her head. "That was for my benefit, not yours. A reminder of the truth, no matter my conflicting emotions or circumstances."

"And evidence that you're pursuing the Lord, not running from him." Cash leaned forward and grasped the bar on which she sat, sandwiching her between his gloved hands. "I'm sorry I hurt you with my careless words this past week. It wasn't my intent." His gaze turned pleading. "Please know that *you* are the treasure I want by my side, Gwynn, not money. You're courageous, talented, honorable, humble—I want you in my life. Give me the chance to earn your trust ... and your heart." He leaned closer still. "And if your heart is set on Boston, then I'm willing to move there too."

Her eyes flared. "I couldn't ask you to do that."

"You're not asking. I'm offering." His gaze darted between her eyes and her mouth, and he whispered, "Whatever it takes to prove myself to you, I'll do it. Please tell me I have a chance."

Take risks. Fall in love. Forgive.

How many more signs did God have to arrange before she abandoned her worries and teenage fallacies and accepted Cash as a worthy suitor? She'd spent almost a decade missing this man— she would not spend the rest of her life in the same manner because she'd bent the knee to fear.

Gwynn hooked her fingers into one of his coat pockets. "Of course you have a chance. Though I'd be lying if I said I didn't trust you already. But can you first forgive me for mishandling the rift between our fathers? For being stubborn and blind even now? I'm sor—"

"Done."

His mouth covered hers in a hungry kiss. She squeaked, momentarily losing her balance on the bar, then grabbed his collar and returned his kiss with as much enthusiasm as he gave.

After a moment, he murmured against her lips, "I don't deserve you."

"Nor I, you." She linked her arms about his neck, his hand at her back persuading her off the jungle gym and into his embrace. "But maybe it's less about what we deserve, and more about what we choose. What we commit to. To whom we choose to commit."

Cash's blue eyes glinted under the brim of his Stetson. "I'm committed to spending the rest of my life convincing you to choose me."

"I don't think it's gonna take that long." And she lifted her face to receive another kiss.

Chapter Thirty-Three

New Year's Eve, Prospect, MT

GWYNN SPOONED potato salad onto her paper plate and eyed the other options of meats, cheeses, fruits, and sweets laid out along the island counter. Ahead of her in line, Gramps snuck his third chocolate cupcake. Behind her, Lainey loaded a plate while detailing her upcoming trip to Europe. Gwynn nodded occasionally, her gaze roaming the Forresters' grandiose living area.

Conversations drifted from different groups assembled on folding chairs or tucked around the dining table or clustered at the foot of the stairs. Sporadic laughter rose from the teenagers playing a dice game at the coffee table. Uncle Russ and Aunt Maude chatted with Uncle Erik and Aunt Dani on a pair of sofas perpendicular to the stone fireplace. And above the mantel, the flat-screen TV showed the mounting excitement in New York City as people counted down the last forty-seven minutes before the annual ball drop.

"…and the dish ran away with the spoon."

Gwynn blinked and turned to her cousin. "The dish did what-now?"

Lainey gave a good-natured groan. "How much did you miss? I knew better than to gush about my plans tonight. You're too spacey."

Gwynn winced. "Sorry." She plucked a biscuit from a straw basket and stepped away from the food. "I'm still a bit shell-shocked. A month ago, I was planning to ring in the New Year like I usually do—alone with the TV and my goldfish, waiting for my suite mates to return from whatever party they'd attended."

"Um, that's depressing."

"But familiar. And safe." Gwynn brought a grape to her lips. "Yet, here I am, celebrating way outside my comfort zone. It's surreal."

Hands slid around her waist from behind. She started, dropping the grape, then relaxed as the telltale mix of spice and wood shavings drifted over her shoulder. Lips grazed her earlobe, shooting off an internal shower of fireworks.

"Have to reassure myself you're real," Cash murmured, his arms tightening, "and not a figment of my imagination."

Gwynn balanced her plate in one hand and laid her other atop his, lacing their fingers together. "You and me, both. Besides the part where Irene fired me, this does have a dreamlike quality to it. Packing up my things and returning to my hometown right after Christmas … Starting a new job with this crazy carpenter—"

"Crazy *hot* carpenter," Cash said, nuzzling her neck.

"Reconciling with family … Definitely the stuff of dreams."

"Mostly because of the hot carpenter, though, right?"

"Mostly because he's letting me splash paint all over his gorgeous creations."

Cash straightened. "I don't remember seeing 'splash' in the contract."

"I don't remember a contract."

"A handshake, then."

Lainey laughed. "It's good to see you two back together. An odd pairing, when you think about it, but love rarely makes sense." She patted Gwynn's arm and moved away, adding, "All is right in my world again."

"Odd pairing?" Cash grumbled. "I think we're perfect."

Gwynn set her plate on the counter and rotated within his arms. She tilted her head back to meet his gaze. "Oddly perfect? Perfectly odd?"

Cash smoothed a strand of hair from her temple and tucked it behind her ear. "What say we take our perfect oddities someplace more private to talk? Front porch sound good to you?"

"It's below zero out there."

He winked. "A few kisses ought to keep us sufficiently warm."

They bundled up, and on their way to the door, Gwynn caught Aunt Dani's gaze. She indicated that she and Cash were stepping outside. Aunt Dani nodded, her eyes creasing in a smile, and returned to her conversation.

"I'm so relieved the Davisons and Forresters are getting along," Gwynn said, traversing the porch with Cash and leaning into the railing. Moonlight highlighted the barn and surrounding fields of the Forresters' small farm.

Although Erik and Dani had rejoiced when they learned Gwynn was alive, they envied the years Maude and Russ had maintained a relationship with her. Those first few encounters between the two couples would have made Jack Frost freeze. But Gwynn trusted God would fully restore their friendships.

A bleat came from one of the goats in the barn. She propped an elbow on the handrail and faced Cash, her cheeks already stinging from the cold. "Remember our last New Year's Eve together?"

He mirrored her stance with a saucy grin. "We made out in your barn's hay loft."

Gwynn quirked an eyebrow. "We watched the fireworks our nearest neighbors were shooting off."

"Hmm." He removed his gloves then pulled the mitten from her hand resting on the railing. "I don't recall that part."

Frigid air danced atop her skin. "Why am I not surprised?"

"Now that we won't be trespassing, we should reenact the making out part." He lifted her hand and kissed her fingertips, one at a time.

Her stomach swirled, and heat blazed along her limbs, chasing away the chill. "A little more than three months until I turn twenty-five and the ranch is legally mine."

"What did the Davisons say about your idea to sell the property and gift them part of the profits?" Cash slid his fingers between hers, and her skin tingled.

"You were right—they *vehemently* rejected it. Like, I have a new appreciation for the 'shooting daggers' idiom. I almost suffered lacerations."

He laughed. "I'd say 'I told you so,' except you already admitted as much."

"I can't live at the ranch, Cash."

"I know."

"So, I came up with a new idea."

He cocked his head as if to say, *Tell me more.*

"What if I subdivided the property, sold the portion with the house, and kept the other portion for myself? Or for a future investment? With the profits from the house sale, I could build a cabin and use some of the land's timber for projects at the Plane & Knotty."

Cash opened his mouth, but Gwynn put her free hand to his lips. "Or I could sell the property as-is, or still sub-divide and sell, but regardless, I could take the profits to help you buy out Gramps and expand your business. *Or* maybe I gift money to Ainsley for college." She lowered her hand. "What do you think?"

"I think I'm about to add to your heap of ideas." He crooked his finger through one of her belt loops. "I finally heard back from a collector regarding the Confederate and US bills that are in decent condition." He tugged on the belt loop. "She's interested in buying them for a fair price, if you're interested in selling."

Gwynn caught her bottom lip in a smile. "So ... we have several options."

Cash walked his hand around to the back of her waist. "I like the sound of 'we.' Does this mean you're still considering me a part of your future?"

"You know I am."

"Good. 'Cause I have something for you." Straightening, he laid his gloves on the railing, dug into his jeans' pocket, and withdrew a chain necklace. A silver cage pendant dangled from it. Reaching around her neck to clasp the chain, he looked into her eyes. "The next piece of jewelry I give you will involve an insane amount of bling. But for tonight"—he ran his hands down her arms—"I thought this was more appropriate."

Intrigued, Gwynn lifted the pendant and squinted at the small object inside the wire cage. Her eyebrows rose. "The bullet that was lodged in my peacoat."

Cash nodded. "Its purpose is twofold. First, to remind you that God still has a plan for you, and you're not worthless, no matter how you feel at times. The truth is, you're invaluable—to many people, but especially to me." He fingered the pendant. "And second ..."

She wet her lips. "Yes?"

"I want you to think of this as a type of promise ring. My promise to pursue you with the goal of making it permanent one day—soon, I hope—before God." His hand moved to cup her cheek. "I thought I lost you a decade ago. I almost lost you a few weeks ago. Lord willing, I won't lose you again until we're old and gray and can look back on a life well lived and well loved. Deal?"

Eyes stinging, she slipped her arms around his waist in a hug. "Deal," she murmured against his chest. "You know what else this pendant represents?"

"What?"

"My fears." She gave him a squeeze. "Because now they're caged, and I'm free to dream again."

The Lord had done that for her. She'd begun the month in a complacent daze, not realizing her soul withered in an emotional prison, yet God had moved in both herself and others to help liberate her. Thus, as December drew to a close on a year of "meh," she emerged onto green pastures, her mind whirring with fresh direction, inspiration, and hope for what her future held.

Thank you, Lord, for answering the prayers I didn't know—or forgot— I had.

One being the man in her arms.

Gwynn snuggled into Cash. *This is the start of something wonderful.*

"I couldn't agree more." Lifting her chin, Cash trailed his lips along her jawline to her mouth. "Now, if you would quit thinking out loud and kiss me …"

Epilogue

New Year's Eve, Flitterndorf

KRIS KRINGLE gazed down at his growing family from his stance at the loft railing. From the littlest ones playing with their toy cars by the fireplace hearth in the living room to the older ones in the kitchen fixing a snack to tide everyone over until midnight, four generations of Kringles talked, laughed, played, or dozed downstairs.

Strong individuals, each of them, the younger adults having already shown their courage and determination a few years before. But what about the newest generation of Kringles—fragile, innocent, brimming with wonder and delight? They entered a world teetering on the brink of madness, where the idea of "goodwill to men" meant nothing to those who rejected its message. Would these youngsters stand strong against the growing tide, or be swept away?

Kris's wife, Anne, ascended the spiral staircase and joined him at the railing. "For one about to welcome in a New Year, you look decidedly un-jolly. What troubles you?"

He draped an arm around her shoulders and pulled her close. "There's a change coming, my dear," he murmured, stroking his beard. "Last week on my flight around the world, I noticed a shift in the believers' lights. Countries that had consistently burned brightest have dimmed drastically, while those countries where few lights used to shine slowly gain in intensity. But the darkness is vast, Anne, and it seethes with barely restrained evil." He pressed his cheek against her braided hair. "What will our great-grandchildren be forced to endure by the time they're ready to take up the Kringle mantel?"

"They shall not be left without aid, Kris. The Christmas Spirit will be here to guide them, you need not fear. Like all Kringles before them, they were born at the right time for their purpose in time." She patted his back. "I take it your assignment in America did not go as planned?"

His gaze went to Gwynn's painting temporarily placed on the mantel. "On the contrary, it was a success. Lost hearts found healing and forgiveness and rediscovered love. I played but a small part, in truth. The catalyst, if you will." He winked. "Although, I may have swirled the waters a time or two."

"Small part or big part, we each play *a* part. It might take us across the world or no farther than Flitterndorf's borders. It might come with a high level of influence or the simpler task of loving our neighbors well." She wagged a finger at him. "But no one is meant to carry *all* the world's burdens, even someone bearing the Kringle namesake. We must yield to the guidance of the Christmas Spirit. It's He who does the heavy-lifting, dearest, not you."

The weighty band that had seized his heart for the past month broke free at his wife's words, and Kris took a deep, cleansing breath.

He let it out again with a soft *ho, ho, ho.* "Who am I to be so blessed with such a wise woman? You've soothed my soul, Anne Kringle." He kissed her upturned lips then tucked her arm into the crook of his elbow. "Let us go down and ring in the New Year with the brightest little lights of the future."

Acknowledgments & Notes

Writing is a solitary venture. At first. But after that initial draft or two, if one seeks to present a well-crafted book to the world, writing requires lots of comments, suggestions, opinions, and critiques from other trusted sources, be they other writers or voracious readers.

So, thank you to my local writing group, The Scribblers, and my online critique group, The Storyteller Squad, without whom this book would probably still be languishing in my laptop, in constant editing mode.

Thanks, especially, to Leah Schwabauer, who listens to my frustrations, reads my cringey second drafts, prays during my lows, and exalts during my highs. As I've said before, I can't wait to be *your* cheerleader! Thank you, Robyn Hook, for your honesty and suggestions on my early draft. I value our friendship and your insights. Thank you, Tiffany Olson, Mindy Peltier, Lea Freitas, Braelyn Germaine, Gretchen Carlson, Kristen Johnson, and Carol Eaton for being willing to read and comment and critique at different stages of this book's journey. Thank you, Detective Bob, for a fun conversation over coffee and helping me figure out what would and would not work in my plot line. (Any plot mishaps in this novel are the fault of my own, not Detective Bob!)

A big thank you to my hubby, as well, who has supported my writing dreams, encouraged me despite my doubts, and prayed me through my slumps. If some of you questioned Cash's patience and ability to forgive in the pages of this story, I pulled from real life, for though my hubby has his faults (don't we all!), he's an amazing man of God and is far more patient and loving than I deserve. I am such a blessed woman.

And last but never least, I thank my Lord and Savior, Jesus Christ, for blessing me with fresh ideas when I dug out this old WIP (work-in-progress) over a year ago. Hubby has been unemployed the entire time I've been working on this revamped story, but God knew what would keep me from descending into the depression wastelands: continued creative inspiration. This WIP has gone through so many renditions over the last two decades— yep, two—as I've pulled it out, worked on it, mulled it over, put it away again. I loved the characters but no longer loved the plot line, so when God planted the seed to give the story a Christmas theme (of *course*! *facepalm*), I was off and running.

Admittedly, I took some liberties off the pages of the Bible. In Acts 8:26-40, God used Philip to share the good news about Jesus to a eunuch. As soon as Philip finished baptizing the eunuch, the Spirit took him away to another town. Given that my version of Santa Claus is used by the Lord, I figured he, too, could be spirited away at times. Hence why Gwynn sees him one minute … and then he's gone in the next.

In Luke 24:13-35, we have the account of two disciples walking along the road to Emmaus, discussing the events surrounding Jesus's death and supposed resurrection. Jesus joins them on the road and opens their spiritual eyes to the Scriptures regarding the Messiah, but they are prevented from recognizing Him with their physical eyes until later, when they're sharing a meal with Jesus. If you've read accounts from missionaries over the centuries, you know that God still conceals man's vision at times for His purposes. Hence why, for the purposes of my story, Cash is briefly prevented from recognizing Gwynn.

Liberties aside, I'm delighted to share Gwynn & Cash's story with you, at long last. I'm also delighted to have dived back into

Christian romance, the genre through which I originally honed my skills. My faith is inextricable from my daily life, my daily thoughts, that it's hard *not* to infuse a story with a faith-based thread.

But whether my future titles include more Christmas fantasy, Christian romances, or something else, I'm hopeful the Lord has a few more books in me yet. ☺

About the Author

LAURIE GERMAINE is the author of the YA Christmas fantasy romances, *Tinsel in a Tangle* and *Tinsel in a Twist*. As a New England native, she once dreamed of raising a family in Europe, but thankfully God knew what her heart truly desired. She now lives quite happily in Montana with her husband of twenty-four years, their two daughters, three horses, a sweet Alaskan Malamute, and a revolving number of chickens. When not immersed in writing or reassessing her role as mom and homemaker to her almost-grown children, you can find her knitting, working on random crafts around the home, and dreaming of a white Christmas.

Also by Laurie Germaine

Tinsel in a Tangle

In the arctic town of Flitterndorf, generations of elves have worked alongside generations of Kringles to make gifts for believing children worldwide. But never have they endured a tall, blundering elf like Tinsel. Despite her setbacks, Tinsel is determined to prove her worth by nabbing an internship at the Workshop. When her chemistry lab explodes, however, destroying gift reserves and putting Christmas in jeopardy, she lands a punishment mucking reindeer stalls for Santa's hotshot grandson, Niklas.

Now if she wants a second chance at that position, she must collaborate with the twinkle-eyed flirt to redeem herself in everyone's eyes without messing up. For one more mishap will not only bring about the holiday's demise, but she'll be immortalized as the elf who shattered children's faith in Santa Claus.

So not the way she wants to go down in history.

Tinsel in a Twist

It's been almost two years since Christmas elf, Tinsel, joined the Minor Flight Team and started dating Niklas Kringle, Santa's grandson. But during a practice flight, she unintentionally endangers the reindeer and gets suspended from the job she loves. When Santa's age-old enemy, Krampus, threatens a Christmas takeover, Tinsel seizes the opportunity to win back everyone's trust *and* her position. For the key to Krampus's downfall lies halfway around the world in a legendary Silver Reindeer, and Tinsel alone has the talent for reindeer speech.

Once overseas, however, Tinsel runs into Niklas's ex-fiancée, Gretel (who may still have designs on becoming his Mrs. Kringle), and discovers that not only has the Silver Reindeer disappeared, but so has her talent. Now rendered useless against Krampus, and outclassed by Gretel, Tinsel must devise a new plan to save the futures of Christmas, her love life, and her career, before they unravel faster than a trio of ugly sweaters.

This is *so* not the most wonderful time of the year.